About the Author

J A Ryan was born in Sean Ross Abbey, Roscrea, Ireland on April 20th, 1969. When she was three weeks old, she was transported to Stamullen Mother and Baby home in County Meath where she was adopted.

She grew up in a loving, secure environment. She had a typical rural Ireland village childhood of horse riding and playing tennis (the latter developing so that in her teens she played in various tournaments around Ireland).

Due to scarcity of work she left Ireland in her early twenties to live and work in London for many years, where she met her husband. She finally settled down in the Northwest of England and has one child. She works alongside her husband in building up their internet business.

From an early age she knew she was adopted. As the years went by, she grew very curious about her identity and her start in life. She felt incomplete. She had a need to find out about her history.

She is a very keen runner and has completed the Manchester marathon. Running and training for the marathon is what got her through the stresses of tracing her birth mother. It helped her deal with the restrictions of the Irish Legal System and the governing bodies.

This memoir is J A Ryan's first memoir. It highlights the difficulties she endured from the government agencies and the Irish legal system in trying to discover her identity. Also, in trying to locate her birth certificate. A document that is rightfully hers.

Prologue

Throughout my life, I have always been determined. I have always cared about what people thought of me and felt a need to prove myself – from my teenage passion for competitive tennis to, much more recently, marathon running.

When I was younger, I felt I had to prove myself to my adoptive father. I really loved that man. I wanted so desperately for him to be proud of me, and the only way I felt that I could do this was to win everything I could. Whenever I came second, I felt that I had subtly failed him.

The crucial part was this: it wasn't my dad putting me under pressure to win, it was me. I knew, deep down, that he was always proud of me. It just took me a long time to realise it.

The search for my birth mother, however, took the need for determination to a whole new level.

I have had to jump over so many hurdles, many deliberately placed before me by the Irish legal system and by those individuals who enforce it. I've been urged and encouraged to quit. I've had obstacles put in my path. I've even been shown the door by a priest, who told me to "be grateful" for what I had. Yet I still hungered to know the history of my past.

This is the story of that search.

And its message is simpler still: to never give up.

Chapter 1

I have known all my life that I was adopted. My adoptive parents, my mum and dad, told me when I was very young. I don't have a recollection of when that was, exactly. I have always known.

For a long time — for my whole life so far — I have felt like a part of me is missing, or that I wasn't "whole". I have wanted some questions answered, about my history, and about the woman who brought me into this world.

I have always known this much: Mum and Dad could not have children of their own, so they decided to adopt. They adopted my sister first, then me, and finally my brother. My dad loved children. Well, they both did.

Growing up I always felt different. I was very shy and lacking in confidence. I was adopted into a large extended Irish family. Maybe I was a little overwhelmed by this, even though both my immediate and my extended family were loving and inclusive. We three were made to feel as if we were blood-related; and we were – and remain – very close. There were fifteen in my mother's family and six in my father's. So, you can just imagine the numbers of cousins I have, in various parts of the world – I can't keep up with them all!

So, it is a puzzle. I grew up in a secure family environment where I was accepted by everyone, but I still felt subtly different, as if I didn't quite belong. It is a hard thing to put into words. As I type this, I feel bad for even feeling the way I do because I had such a privileged upbringing. We didn't want for anything. My mum and dad were always there for me.

However, they are not my birth parents – even though I would love it if they were! So, the mystery of my birth parents disturbs me. I always sensed that there was a lot of my history I didn't know about. I knew all about my adoptive parent's history: where they came from, all about my adoptive grandparents, all the family secrets. I felt 100% a part of the family. At the back of my mind — though — there was always a sense of being on the outside, looking in.

It wasn't the family that made me feel this way. It was the fact that I always knew, from my earliest thoughts, that I needed to know where I came from and what the first three weeks of my life were like.

This feeling — always powerful — has grown even stronger over the last two years since I started my search. I also know that my urge to find out the truth about myself is far from unique. I've read many stories and articles where people in similar situations, even those from similarly loving backgrounds, had the same feelings and insecurities.

I realise that this is difficult to understand, and that I may come across as contradicting myself, or even as ungrateful and selfish – considering what my parents have done for me! However, the truth is quite the opposite. My parents mean the world to me, and I wouldn't do anything to hurt them. What I felt about needing to find my past is, for this reason, very difficult to explain.

Even as a child I often thought about my birth mother. I often wondered why she had given me away and whether I looked like her. Sometimes I cried myself to sleep thinking about her and singing the song "Nobody's Child" in my head. I suppose a part of me still felt unwanted and rejected, as if a little piece of me was always missing. I never spoke about these feelings. I kept them all bottled up inside me.

Maybe that wasn't such a good idea because, as the years went by, I started drinking. I suppose drinking was my way of trying to forget the missing part of my life. When I was twenty-three, I left home and moved to England. I drank my way through my twenties. I really don't remember a lot of it. My mind was very messed-up. I felt as if I was two different people. I think I was finding not knowing my true identity increasingly difficult to deal with.

I guess — even twenty years ago — I was on a quest, perhaps to find my birth mother? Perhaps, to find me.

Chapter 2

This need to know my history became so overwhelming that I decided that I had to trace my birth mother. The journey that followed was not as smooth as I'd hoped: I encountered numerous hurdles along the way.

The first step was to register with the Irish Child and Family Centre. This government agency (known as TUSLA) was first set up on January 1st, 2014. It was dedicated to improving wellbeing and outcomes for children. The government holds the records for all adoptees in Ireland and operates in every region throughout the country.

I also looked up on the internet what rights I had (if any) about obtaining my information. There I found out that, under international law, adopted people have the right to establish their identity – except in some countries, including Ireland. There, as a result of a 1998 Supreme Court Ruling, those adopted through Mother and Baby Homes or similar Catholic institutions were prevented access to adoption and birth records, in order to protect the privacy of the mother. This meant that consent from the birth parents was required in order for an adopted person to view his or her birth records.

In addition to registering with the Irish government, I also put my name on the National Adoption Contact Preference Register, in Dublin. The Register was set up in 2005 as a way for people affected by adoption to make their wishes known about contact with their birth family. I was advised by a friend to do this. In his words, "You never know – something might turn up!"

Before starting my search, in June 2014, I needed to get a copy of my non-identifying information. When I contacted the Irish government by email, they sent me this information by post. The non-identifying information I received referred only to me, including: the name given me by my adoptive parents, my date of birth, my weight at birth, my immunisations, the date I was placed with my adoptive parents and the fact I was a premature baby. It was all extremely basic information, and the information relating to my birth parents was equally minimal. It gave their ages, occupation and religion. Any identifying details were redacted (for example, my birth mother's signature).

After receiving my non-identifying information, I contacted TUSLA and made them aware that I wished to trace my birth mother and at that point I was assigned a social worker. Her name was Mary.

Chapter 3

I grew up in an idyllic village in Catholic Ireland. It had two rows of terraced houses, and in the middle was what we called The Green. The Green ran the length of the entire village, forming its centrepiece. At either end there were ponds, where, as kids, we used to fish for tadpoles with our fishing nets. One end featured an old water pump, which is still there. There was an incredibly old stone monument in the middle section, which used to be our base when playing tag.

It had a pub, a post office, a chemist's and the three corners of the village boasted shops, one of which was ours. In fact, that corner of the village was even named after us! My mum and dad had bought the two-storey detached house, shop and land before I was born. One of my earliest memories is of the house being knocked down and the bungalow, my home, being built. I have memories of climbing over slats of wood that were lying in the huge hallway when I was only two years old. I remember living in the dingy, dark store section while the build was going on. I'm sure there were mice in there!

I loved our house. We had a big four-bedroom detached bungalow. When I was little, the main hallway appeared massive to me. It was painted white and looked very bright and airy. When you opened the dark wooden front door, you could see a wide-open space with a piano stored in an alcove on the left-hand side. There was an old grandfather clock at the end of the hall opposite the front door. We all had our own bedrooms. Mine had two single beds, a built-in wardrobe and a big desk at which I did my schoolwork. I used the hallway to practice my gymnastics routines for school.

The kitchen-diner was quite large, with a picture of Jesus on the wall with a little red light on the bottom of it. (I don't think that light ever worked!) When we were little, we used to kneel down in front of the living room furniture every night and say the Rosary. We attended mass every Sunday without fail, and we even used to have visits from the parish priest. Father Abbott was his name: such a nice man. I wonder now if all of this was part of the adoption process and if he was keeping tabs on all of us.

I have fond memories of my childhood. Growing up in a village was fantastic. I couldn't have asked for a better upbringing. My dad was popular in the area and very well-liked. I suppose owning a shop you are bound to be known, but people used to come into the shop just to have a chat with my dad, not simply to buy something. The children in the village loved him. He used to have the craic with them. He was so

popular that, when he died, the children in the community held a guard of honour for him the whole length of the village. (What a moving sight!)

Sunday mornings were the best. When we went to ten o'clock Mass with my mother, we would visit my aunt and uncle afterwards. They lived across the road from the church and owned a shop. It wasn't just us visiting aunts, cousins. . . it was a family event. We used to get sweets in the shop, as well. Arriving home from ten o'clock Mass was also wonderful: I will never forget the aromas in that kitchen. Mummy would have roast chicken in the oven and an apple tart just ready to be baked. My favourite memory of Sunday morning was when she'd let me have the crispy skin off the chicken: yum! And when my dad and I pulled the wishbone together and made our wishes. (I have carried on that tradition with my son to this day!)

My dad also owned land at the back of the house, a yard with sheds and a barn. Beyond that yard was our field. He used to house suckling calves and lambs in those sheds. Daddy also had Granny's land, where he kept livestock. When I was a little girl, I remember he brought home an orphaned baby lamb that needed to be bottle-fed. He gave her to me, and I named her Bluebell. We also looked after the suckling calves. My dad used to say, "Put your hand in its mouth and it will suck on it" – and it always did.

Dad also made a swing for me, hanging it from the highest rafter in the barn. We also had a field where all the children in the village could wander off on adventures. We used to jump the ditches into the neighbouring land. There was an orchard at the other end of the village, where we used to trespass and nick the apples. Heaven help us if we got caught – but we had great adventures!

As I grew older, I became more and more interested in tennis. That was my love throughout my teens. Mum used to drive me to the various tournaments: some I won, some I lost. I used to take over the TV in our sitting-room for the whole two weeks of Wimbledon every year. I watched all the matches, and the highlights. John McEnroe was my hero.

I also liked to ride. My brother had a pony and I used to ride out whenever he'd let me. I went on a few hunts and rode with my cousin, on my uncle's land. As my brother got more and more into horses, my dad converted his sheds into stables so that all the young kids in the area could house their ponies there. It was a hobby for my dad, who loved both horses and people. He also set up horse jumps in the field, where my brother used to have show jumping competitions.

Growing up, I was always told by a neighbour that she remembered the day Mummy and Daddy brought me home from Stamullen. She remembered how tiny I was and how proud Daddy was. He had adopted his second child. I was his. He had two daughters now. There is a story, which my sister has often told, about her wanting to

drown me. You see, I was in my pram outside the shop door. (Yes, that is what they did back then. They left the babies in the prams to get some fresh air. You wouldn't do it now!) My sister, then only three, was very jealous of me. So, she decided to push me in my pram across the road to the Green. She was heading for the pond when my mum caught her. She wanted to drown me because she didn't like me. She was jealous of all the attention I was getting. Sisterly love, eh?!

I also remember sleepovers in my various cousins' houses. Staying up past midnight playing Monopoly. Holidays down the country and abroad. We were, and still are, such a close-knit family! Looking back, I can see how privileged I was, to have been adopted into my family, both immediate and extended. And, believe me, I wouldn't have changed any of it for the world.

It wasn't all rosy in the garden, though. There were a couple of people in the family who didn't see my brother, my sister and me as 100% family. One aunt, on my mother's side, always treated me as second-best. She always compared me to my cousin. Grades at school, exam results, career choices: she always looked down her nose at me, though not so much now, as I have a family of my own, including a sixteen-year-old doing really well at school. My husband and I also have a successful business. My cousin, on the other hand, is single, going out with a divorced, much older, man and doesn't have any children.

It's funny how things turn out.

There was also an uncle on my dad's side, now deceased, who I always thought accepted us: turned out I was wrong.

That story starts when my granny died. My dad looked after the land and livestock, as my uncle wasn't physically able. Dad put a lot of time and money into that land over many years. He had a "gentleman's agreement" with my uncle that he'd take care of the land and, if my dad died before my uncle, that the land would pass down to my brother. Well, that didn't happen. Then, when my uncle died, after my dad, we learned that he'd left the land to a cousin, someone who had nothing to do with the land. It is believed my uncle didn't leave the land to my brother because he wasn't blood-related, but "only" adopted.

So: there you have it. My uncle couldn't even follow through with a promise he'd made to my father, partly because of his religious beliefs, partly because of what society dictated to him when he was a young man and partly because – at the end of the day – he believed us to be second-class citizens, simply because we were adopted. We weren't true family. How narrow-minded people can be! This was all quite upsetting for my brother and me, as we always believed we had been accepted by everybody.

Even in the 21st century, the Catholic Church still has a profound influence on the older generation. However, what I still cannot understand is why my uncle betrayed my father's wishes, after everything my dad had done for him over the years. And the sad part was that he betrayed him because, in his eyes and in the eyes of the church, we were illegitimate – adopted or not.

Chapter 4

Back in 1992, now a staggering 25 years ago, I travelled to London in search of work, as the job situation in Ireland was pretty grim. I worked in the centre of London and lived in the southwest of the city.

One hot sunny Saturday in May 1998, a group of us went to a sports bar on the Kings Road in London. We were there to have lunch before watching the FA Cup Final between Arsenal and Newcastle. There were twelve of us at the lunch table and I sat next to a guy I'd never met before, a friend of my ex-boyfriend's. We talked and talked and just seemed to instantly hit it off. This guy is now my husband.

After a little indecision on Max's part we finally got together. He was unsure of asking me out because of my ex but I reassured him it was okay. I even got my ex to tell him so!

While this was going on, I was desperately grieving the sudden death of my father. Dad had died only two months before I met Max, so the grief was still quite raw. I was at my lowest point ever. Drinking myself into oblivion was the only thing I was interested in doing: nothing else mattered. My father had always meant the world to me. Also, I hadn't been with him when he died: it took me a long time to get over that. Max stuck with me and helped me out of my dark place. He turned my life around, helped build up my confidence and restored my self-belief. It must have been love because he could so easily have walked away. If it weren't for Max, I'm not sure where I would be today.

I was also in the process of buying my first flat, a two-bedroomed flat in southwest London. I moved into it in the July of 1998. Max and I were seeing quite a lot of each other by then, so much so that, by the time November rolled around, I had moved into his flat in south London and rented out my own. Fast movers, I hear you say!

I loved living with Max in his one-bedroomed ground-floor flat. It was warm and cosy, our little haven. It was so nice to come in from work in the evenings and shut the rest of the world out!

In January 1999 Max and I got engaged. Max proposed – well, it wasn't a proposal, as such. One Sunday morning when we were driving around Chiswick looking for bagels, we were stopped at a set of traffic lights in Max's Renault Megane and he said to me, "Why don't we get married?"

And there you have it. The most romantic proposal ever . . . not!

In our early thirties, we both had good jobs in London: I worked in the City and Max in Fulham. As soon as we got engaged, we started talking about moving out of London and starting a family – I suppose I was conscious of my biological clock.

We decided to get married in the November of 1999 and to relocate to the northwest in mid-December. Ideally, I'd have liked to have moved back to Ireland, as all my family were there, but my husband wanted to stay close to his mum: she would have been on her own otherwise. So, we sold two flats – that wasn't difficult to do; they were snapped up – moved up north and haven't looked back since. Our son, Alex, arrived in late August 2000.

We were married in Kiliney Bay, south Dublin. What a beautiful place – and what a wedding to remember! We must have done well, because people still comment on what a great day it was. I was only home for a funeral, a couple of weeks ago, when my cousin mentioned in conversation what a great wedding ours had been. She was still commenting on it, seventeen years later! I think the success of that day was down to the good mix of guests. We had fifty percent Irish, while the other half was made up of English, Australians and Americans. Also, we got married on a Thursday and spent the long weekend in Dublin with our friends. The honeymoon came later. A good percentage of our wedding guests were family, whether cousins, aunts, uncles etc. These people wanted to be there with me to celebrate my big day and I wanted them there. These are the people I call family. Blood relations simply don't define a family unit!

When I started writing this book, I asked Max if he remembered when I told him that I was adopted. He didn't. He also said 'Why would I remember when it didn't impact on my life? The fact that you're adopted doesn't alter the way I feel about you!' Max has been so supportive throughout my journey – throughout all my journeys. I was so lucky to find him!

Chapter 5

In June 2014 I decided to do some detective work myself. If you recall, all I had to go on was my non-identifying information, as the law prevented me from accessing anything else without my birth mother's consent.

So, I flew to Dublin to visit the General Register Office, basing myself at my mums for a couple of days.

I took a bus to Heuston Station and then a taxi to the GRO. The taxi driver was a lovely man. Very chatty, he advised me to be extremely careful in that part of Dublin, and to be on my guard, as there were drug dealers and addicts active in the area. When I got out of the car I felt uneasy, but I managed to find the General Register Office quickly.

I'd already been in touch with a friend who was knowledgeable about Irish adoption procedures. I had spoken to him a few days previously and, when I mentioned that I was coming to Dublin, he said that he would meet me in the GRO. With his help I actually found my original birth certificate! What an amazing moment: to hold it in my hands for the first time!

I learned my birth mother's name and the name she had given me. I also learned my place of birth. My birth mother's name was Margaret and my original name had been Catherine. I had been born in Sean Ross Abbey in Roscrea. I just stared at the paper and broke down in tears. My friend put his arm around me and gave me a hug. I was so grateful to him because there was no way I would have obtained this valuable piece of information without him.

I phoned my husband Max straightaway. He was at home looking after our son and our business; I was in Dublin by myself. In hindsight, maybe it wasn't very sensible of me to be on my own, but I'd waited 45 years to receive this information, and I couldn't wait a moment longer. My feelings were of shock, excitement, happiness and a sense of achievement – but also of sadness. The sadness was related to my birth mother's giving me away and to my yearning to find out the reasons why.

At that moment in time my mind was intent upon locating my birth certificate and finding out my identity. Finding out who I was for the first three weeks of my life. Who my birth mother was. What her name was. As time went on I got more and more curious. I wanted to find out the circumstances surrounding my conception and my birth. Who was this Margaret? Was she still alive and living in Ireland? Did I look like her? Did I have any brothers or sisters? Were they my full or half-siblings? I had loads of questions! – and, in order to feel whole, I needed some answers. For 45 years I'd felt that a piece of me was missing. This was my chance to find it.

Shortly after obtaining this information I left the GRO and headed back towards the city centre, to get a bus back to my mum's. I walked through Dublin in a haze, crying. Crying tears of happiness that I had found the information I'd craved for so long – and tears of sadness for the woman who had brought me into the world, and then decided to give me away.

I knew in that moment that I needed to carry on with my search. I needed to learn the truth about my history. I was getting some funny looks from passers-by, but I didn't stop crying. I couldn't stop crying.

My place of birth was Sean Ross Abbey in Roscrea. This had come as a big shock because I'd always believed - and my adoptive parents had been led to believe – that I'd been born in Stamullen in County Meath, where they had adopted me from. (The non-identifying information had been on letter-headed paper from Stamullen). This revelation hit me hard. I didn't want this to be true, because I'd seen the film Philomena and how the young women had been treated by the nuns. It took me some time to digest this fact because I struggled to believe that I could have been born in that awful place.

My mum and sister met me at the bus stop. They could see I had been crying. We went to a café, where I told them of my news. We were creating scenarios as to my birth mother's circumstances. How she had ended up in Sean Ross Abbey – what might have been her fate. I was very emotional: I kept imagining what life must have been like for her. I imagined she had a rough start, what with being pregnant at the age of twenty and going into premature labour. Then being sent to Sean Ross Abbey to give birth. She must have been terrified. Had she realised what was going on? Had my birth father been with her? Was he still around? It amazed me how the imagination could run away with itself!

When I told my mum about Sean Ross Abbey, she was quite upset. She felt let down by the system and the Church; she felt that she had been deceived and lied to for all these years. Not only in relation to my place of birth but also in relation to my brother and sister's beginnings. It was at this point I knew I had to find the answers to all my questions. I wanted to know what happened to my birth mother and how she ended up in that institution. (Also, had she made it out of there?)

I flew back to England that evening. What a day it had been! – I had lots to think about. After a few days I emailed my social worker Mary, at TUSLA, with this new data. She refused to confirm that what I had discovered was correct. All she could say was "I'm not at liberty to say". As a result, I had to wait 18 months longer for confirmation. During that time, I was left to doubt that the data I had received was correct. This only made me more determined to prove that the information was correct.

As I truly believed it was.

Chapter 6

As I wrote in my diary: My family and I have come back to Ireland for our annual holiday. We come over every year to be with my mum and other family members. The Irish lot as we call them. When we come across, we bring the car, so we can drive around, and Max and Alex can see Ireland. It is such a beautiful country! I have always wanted my son to learn about Ireland and to experience it first-hand.

We came over in August for a week. During that week we planned on going to Sean Ross Abbey and seeing the Mother and Baby Home and the grounds surrounding it. I did remember seeing it in *Philomena*, but I wanted to see it in the cold light of day. After all I had been born there. As mentioned earlier, I had only discovered this piece of information the previous June, upon visiting the General Register Office in Dublin. To have seen in that film how badly the women were treated made me think about my birth mother and what she might have gone through. Just to think that I'd been born in that institution, surrounded by those evil nuns! It made me feel sad and angry to think that vulnerable, naive young women could be treated so badly. I also found it hard to believe that a religious order could institutionalise and degrade women and children the way they did.

We set off on an overcast day from my mum's house: Max drove Alex and me while my sister drove my mum. The drive took an hour and a half. When we arrived at Sean Ross Abbey we drove along a driveway until we came to the main building. As soon as I got out of the car I shivered: I suddenly felt chilled all over. My mind was all over the place. I had the scenes from *Philomena* and images of my birth mother rushing around my head. I had images of my birth mother giving birth to me in the hospital wing in 1969. I pictured her delivering me without any pain relief and being terrified as she probably hadn't known what was going on with her body. You see, back then childbirth was no topic for conversation. She wouldn't have been told what to do or what to expect before, during or after giving birth. She was only 20, left to fend for herself in that godawful place.

I started to cry, because I couldn't bear thinking about the cruelties that had occurred behind those walls. I cried not only for my birth mother but also for those other women who had fallen victim to the nuns and society. It was hard to comprehend how badly one human being could treat another, simply for falling pregnant out of wedlock. What gave those nuns the right to abuse the women in the way they did? They weren't solely responsible for getting pregnant. It does take two! – but in Catholic Ireland in the 60s, the focus was on the women even though, according to the Bible, it is a sin for anyone to have sexual intercourse outside of marriage. Despite this, the women got the blame. The men always walked away with reputation intact, even though they could conceivably have impregnated any number of women. Mind-blowing!

We walked around the outside of the main building, as the inside wasn't open to the public. Then we walked towards the graveyard, where we visited the grave of Anthony Lee. Anthony Lee was the young boy depicted in the true story about *Philomena*. He had been adopted by an American couple through the nuns at Sean Ross Abbey. When he was dying, he requested that he be buried there. As we were walking, I was explaining the history and significance of Sean Ross Abbey to Alex. The relevance it had to me. We strolled past a church in ruins and arrived at a gate to a graveyard. On the other side of the gate we could see the graves where the nuns were buried. They had headstones on individual graves.

We carried on along the path and came to a grassy area, hidden and out of the way. This area is known as the Little Angels plot. It is well-maintained with some markings on graves and a stone cross at its centre. Flowers had been placed at the foot of this cross, presumably because visitors hadn't known where their loved ones had been buried. This piece of land is tucked away and not easy to find.

When we came to this plot, I became very emotional. As I walked around, I read the inscriptions on the wooden crosses placed into the grass around the edge of the plot. The inscriptions mentioned how young some of the dead mothers had been. As young as fourteen! I was overwhelmed with grief for the mothers and babies who had lost their lives in that horrible institution. I also had an eerie, sickening feeling that I was walking on a mass grave. How many babies, children and young women were buried under my feet? Why were their graves left unmarked? Why weren't they given a proper burial and headstone to show they were human beings who had once lived in this world, albeit for a short time? Why weren't they treated with dignity and respect? This was all so wrong. . . These people weren't second-class citizens. They weren't pieces of meat. They were like you and me and our children. They deserved so much more!

I left the Little Angels plot feeling dejected, angry and sad, thinking about what those poor, poor women went through. As I was walking on the plot, I thought about my birth mother. *Was she still alive or was she buried in that mass grave? Would I ever find her and get the answers to my questions?*

It was an August day in Roscrea but for me it felt like a cold winter's day in December. I couldn't stop shivering. I felt permanently cold, thinking about the cruelties those poor women endured at the hands of the nuns. Had my birth mother suffered at the hands of those evil people? My mind was about to explode with the mountain of questions that needed answering!

We drove to a pub in Roscrea to get a coffee. We all needed to sit down and absorb what we had been exposed to. We sat in silence. My mum was struggling to understand why and how the Catholic Church could allow such horrific abuse to happen to those poor, unfortunate, vulnerable and naive women. I was finding it hard to comprehend what had gone on behind the closed doors of Sean Ross Abbey all those years ago.

I sat amongst my family, feeling incredibly grateful to my birth mother for giving me away so I could enjoy the privileged life I've had. But most of all appreciating my mum and dad – for choosing me.

Chapter 7

It has been eight months since I flew to Dublin's General Register Office, where I obtained my birth mother's true identity. It has also been eight months since I've spoken to my social worker, Mary.

Funnily enough, I had a phone call from her today, out of the blue, with an update on proceedings.

She told me that she had found two women with the same name. You see, my birth mother's name is quite common in Ireland, both her first and her last names. So, you can imagine all the difficulties. One woman had been eliminated straightaway as she did not fit all the criteria: she was ten years older than the age on the non-identifying information. I wasn't even sure why Mary had told me about this woman, as she wasn't someone she was going to pursue. I guessed it was just part of the process.

The second woman had given two names on the forms: the long version of her name on the admissions form and the shorter version on the consent form. When I looked at the copies, I could see that a longer and a shorter version of her name had been redacted. Her first name could very easily be shortened.

But Mary seemed to think that the woman had given a false name. She mentioned cases where young and frightened women had chosen to give false names upon entering these institutions, so their true identities could never be known.

At first this sounded a bit far-fetched to me. But after giving it some thought, I could picture those poor frightened women living in fear of being shamed for their actions, for committing a mortal sin in the eyes of Catholic Ireland. However, in this case I was unconvinced because I knew both names that she had used.

Her name was Margaret, or Maggie. I had discovered this when I visited the GRO and received a copy of the entry in the official ledgers. I had already tried to tell Mary this, but she chose to ignore me. She refused to admit that any information I had managed to collate by myself was true. She just went along at her own pace, dealing with issues one at a time, sometimes not seeing the obvious. This way of doing things was very frustrating for me. It wasted a lot of time and caused unnecessary stress, in my opinion.

Anyway, back to this woman with two names. Mary contacted the parish priest in the locality where this woman had lived in 1969, to see if he could check out the address that she had left on her forms upon entering Sean Ross Abbey. The priest approached a family at the address, but they denied any knowledge of the woman.

Mary wasn't sure if the family genuinely didn't know her, or if they were covering up for her.

So, we had two women with the same name – and the first had been eliminated. I kept hoping that something might materialise with regards to the second. As the phone call ended, I had a thrill of excitement sweep over me. I wasn't sure what the next step might be, as I was not privy to any of the information on my file, but Mary was actively trying to find her – albeit going a long-winded way about it.

Still, something was moving. There remained a real hope of finding my birth mother, and that was something for me to cling onto.

Chapter 8

After a couple of weeks, I received another phone call from Mary. She was now looking at a third woman with the same name but, and this worried me, someone much younger than the age mentioned on my non-identifying information. However, some of the details match mine. Mary started to talk to me about this woman, though she gave me scenarios, not facts. This woman may have married quite young and was maybe living in the UK. She may have had an affair and returned to Ireland to have the baby without her husband's finding out. She had put the baby up for adoption in Ireland: that was all we knew for sure. Also, the social worker had failed to find her in Ireland, so we would have to try the UK.

I've noticed that whenever Mary phoned with a development, she created scenarios around that information. I asked her to put everything down on an email, so I could access or re-visit the information at any time, but she said that she preferred to talk to me, so that she could better gauge my mood. She liked to get a counselling session in when she phoned up! The trouble with this was that I don't agree with counselling. It might work for some people but it's not for me. I am a strong-minded person, with family and friends to fall back on, if need be.

In fact, I found this way of doing things infuriating because Mary tended to confuse reality with fiction. I thought that I should only be told facts, not possible scenarios, because these scenarios started to play on my mind until sometimes, I wasn't sure what was fact and what was fiction. I sometimes doubted whether Mary knew the difference: she tended to forget what she had told me, and I only had my diaries to refer to. (Luckily, I recorded everything in my diaries, from emails to phone conversations. Otherwise I sometimes wouldn't have known what to believe!)

Most of the time I felt that everything was out of my control, and sometimes that I was unsure which way to turn. Whenever I asked for clarification on something Mary had generally either forgotten that she'd mentioned it or else told me something completely different. I suppose I had to trust that a trained social worker knew what she was doing, but I found myself beating down serious doubts. . . At any rate, the next step was for Mary to contact the DHSS in the UK.

Chapter 9

A couple of weeks have passed since I last spoke to Mary. I am trying to give her a little time to do some investigative work before I ask for any new developments.

It is now the 13th of April 2015, and I've been unwell for a few days. I have been bitten, I think by a horsefly, and have been on a double dose of antibiotics. I have been quite poorly with it and cannot do any training for the half-marathon as my leg has swollen to twice the size it should be. I have also been feeling pretty low. I'm lying on the couch with my leg up when the phone rings. It is Mary's number.

Later: Not good news I'm afraid. This was the last thing I needed to hear today. My low mood just got lower!

Mary told me that she had drawn a blank in the search for the woman in the UK and that she'd have to go back to the drawing board. I was terribly upset, partly because I hadn't seen it coming. Especially, after the phone call a couple of weeks previously, where she had informed me that she had managed to trace a woman of the same name living in the UK. It was so frustrating that I couldn't control my emotions on the telephone. I let Mary know exactly how I was feeling.

It turned out that she was looking at the wrong date of birth for my birth mother. So, all this time she had been searching for a woman with a different birth date to the date listed on my non-identifying information. I mean: this is not rocket science! My mother's age was there, in black and white, on the non-identifying information! I felt quite angry about this. Mary had wasted ten valuable months on false information – something that should have been flagged up much sooner. Surely, she should have noticed the date of birth before now? This is what I meant when I complained before, that she goes off on tangents and follows one lead at a time.

I told her that I was very upset and disappointed, upon which Mary, perhaps in hope, asked me if I wanted to give up the search. I said, "No, I am not giving up!" – and I told Mary not to give up either. I don't give up easily. I was then asked to be patient…that's rich! I have been patient over the last ten months, while she was wasting our time on a complete wild goose chase!

I felt so deflated. Only two weeks before I'd felt upbeat and positive about finding Margaret. Now all of that has been shattered because of a schoolgirl error – of not noticing the date of birth on the papers. *I thought if Mary had only listened to me and taken me seriously when I told her my true identity, we wouldn't be in this position – we'd be a lot further on.* The most maddening part was not the time wasted, but her refusal to listen to me, and her unwillingness to confirm that the information I had was accurate.

As I wrote later, in my diary:

Mary still hasn't acknowledged the information I gave her regarding mine and my birth mother's identity. I am still living in doubt. I am still questioning whether the information from The General Register Office is correct. Deep down, I know it is but there remains an element of doubt when Mary refuses to confirm it. Sometimes she seems to be playing mind games with me. Seeing how strong I am mentally. Every phone conversation ends up being a counselling session. Something I don't want.

This state of "not knowing" was enough to drive anyone insane. She had only to say, "Yes, the information is correct" or "No, it isn't". This doubt undermines any excitement and sense of achievement from discovering any information myself. I vowed that this might get me down but wouldn't keep me down.

I knew in my heart that what I'd found was correct. I just needed to stick to my guns and stay focussed for the prize to be mine. Or so I hoped!

Chapter 10

17 May 2015: A few weeks had passed since that day in April when I had received the devastating news that Mary had hit a brick wall. I supposed that she was in the process of wiping the slate clean and starting from scratch.

While waiting to hear back from her regarding any updates, I decided to try track down my baptismal certificate. After all, experience had proven that I needed to do my own investigative work whenever possible, because the authorities were unlikely to give me any information willingly.

My thinking was that the baptismal certificate should possess the same details as my birth certificate. Also, that I couldn't sit back and wait for TUSLA or the social worker to do their bit. They worked so slowly – one lead at a time. I could be waiting a lifetime for new developments to surface! I decided that I needed to do some snooping around myself. That way I would know, deep down, that at least I had given it my all.

A little research and a few phone calls later, I managed to find out where my baptismal records were held. I phoned the parish priest from the diocese for Sean Ross Abbey in Roscrea and explained what I was looking for. His secretary advised me that the church records for Sean Ross Abbey were held in Kilaloe, in Ennis, County Clare. (I never heard why they were moved. Maybe it was the Church's way of keeping us adoptees from finding out our true identity, to put the records where people would never think to look?)

I immediately phoned the church office in Kilaloe. The lady there was very helpful; and asked me to put my information in an email, promising to get back to me. The only information required was my date of birth, my adopted name, my adoptive parents' names (and address) and the place where I had been adopted. I also supplied my birth mother's name, the name she had given me and my place of birth.

I asked her to kindly confirm that the information I had regarding my birth mother's name was correct; and she told me that it was. I was so relieved to hear this! Over the next few weeks, though, I still found myself doubting whether I had been given the correct information. I found myself watching for the post. I longed to see the facts for myself, in black and white.

Finally, some eight weeks later, I finally received the confirmation I had been waiting for, the formal version of my baptismal certificate. The information on the certificate was identical to the information on my birth certificate, and also to the print-out from the record book in the GRO. So, what I had found out originally and shared with

Mary was true – even though she continued to refuse to confirm it. (The response I inevitably received was, "I'm not at liberty to say".)

As I triumphantly wrote in my diary: *I received my baptismal certificate in the post today, 22nd of July 2015. I feel a real sense of achievement, knowing the information I collated myself in Dublin, back in June 2014, is accurate.*

A couple of days later I phoned Mary, to tell her what I had achieved and to request that she confirm, once and for all, that what I had found out was correct.

She was shocked when I told her what I had done. She could not believe, at least at first, that I had gone looking for the certificate. I think she was also stunned at how easy it had been for me to access the church records. (Really, the only reason I had been given access was because I had all the relevant information to hand: my name and my birth mother's name. For that reason, I think the secretary felt it was OK to give me what was rightfully mine. Thank heavens for decent people!)

What I found especially mind-blowing was that Mary had no idea that the church records for Sean Ross Abbey were held in Killaloe. I struggled with this because, after all, she was supposed to be the professional. This was her job. She really ought to know these things. Surely, if I, only an amateur, could locate these records, she and her office should have been able to? . . . yet it hadn't even entered her head to go down this route. The mind boggled.

I told her that all the information was precisely the same as what I'd already received twelve months earlier from the General Register Office – yet Mary still refused to confirm or deny it. Instead, she was still busy seeding doubts in my head – but two separate sources, surely, couldn't be wrong? I began to feel frustration and anger towards the system and the Church. It was the 21st century, but we were still being treated like second-class citizens.

Every time I made any progress, I was greeted with another hurdle to jump over. All I was asking for was confirmation, but I was still being told "I'm not at liberty to say". Ireland needs to come out of the Dark Ages! We adoptees deserve the right to know our history, to learn who our birth parents are, to discover our identities and to have access to our medical files.

I understood that Mary, and the government too, had to work within the constraints of the law. But surely, if I – the adoptee – had managed to gain legal access to the information by other means they should be willing to confirm or deny its accuracy? Putting me through this uncertainty was inhumane. It was mental cruelty. I had done my own research over a twelve-month period and I believed that what I had learned was true, but I was still left troubled and second-guessing myself.

The law in Ireland rules in favour of the mother, whether dead or alive. The entire system is wrong.

Chapter 11

A few months had passed. We were into September and I still felt that I was being given the brush-off. I had also been emailing Mary and not getting any response. She had been ignoring me ever since July, and I'd gotten to the point where I couldn't take the lack of communication any longer. So, I finally phoned Mary's team leader to complain.

I explained about the breakthrough I'd had with the church records, and how obliging the secretary had been, in confirming that what I already had in hand was correct. I also expressed how irritated and angry I felt at Mary's refusal to admit that everything I had personally discovered was true. I felt that Mary was making me doubt myself, even though there might well be a sense of embarrassment on her side. . . after all, I had found the church records, personally. It hadn't crossed the minds of TUSLA to go there. At the end of the conversation the team leader said that she would speak to Mary and that either she or Mary would get back to me.

Mary called me five days after I had complained about her. She didn't even apologise for the lack of communication, or for the stress that she had caused.

Instead she proceeded to tell me she had been following up a lead on a woman with the same name as my birth mother. She could have emailed me, instead of giving me the silent treatment! Ignoring me only makes my mind wander: I had been thinking all sorts. (Was this all a tacit admission that I had been right all along about the name? Still no confirmation there!) At any rate, Mary had been following up on the woman who went to the UK.

If you cast your mind back to April 2015, Mary had been following up a lead on a younger woman who had moved to the UK. The scenario was – though it was only a scenario – that she'd had an affair, become pregnant and then returned to Ireland to have the baby and to give it up for adoption. Back then, this was nothing more than conjecture. But, at this point Mary was actually suggesting that this woman, now deceased, had been my birth mother.

So, what had changed since April? In April, Mary had told me that she had hit a brick wall with this lead yet now she was telling me, for the second time, no less, that this woman must have been my birth mother. How could she be so certain? – when her date of birth didn't match and when Mary herself had previously been so adamant that this woman was the wrong person? Had Mary uncovered new data, amounting to 100% proof, that this woman was my birth mother – or was she clutching at straws?

As I wrote in my diary: *I am not sure what to believe. I am going along with this, but my gut feeling is telling me she's got hold of the wrong person.*

This younger woman in the UK died shortly before 1998: Mary was not at liberty to give the exact date. She could only tell me that she had died between the years 1993 and 1998, so this woman had died young, in her early fifties, and may have been buried in the UK. Mary had written to the UK for the death certificate, so we should find out the cause of death. If Mary had found the correct woman this would have made her twenty-four or twenty-five when she had me – but, according to my non-identifying information, my birth mother had been twenty when I was born. This simply did not add up, to me. I was unconvinced that they had found the right person. Instead, I was feeling quite confused and a little stressed. I suspected that Mary was on the wrong path yet again.

I had mentioned to Mary that I wanted to know where this woman was buried, so that I could visit her grave. She told me that she was waiting for the death certificate to come in; the place of burial might be on it.

The next step for me would be to retrieve my birth mother's medical records. I also wished to gain access to my file, now that she, assuming she really had been my birth mother was dead.

As I later wrote: *I spoke to my friend today, the 24th of September, about the new developments in my case and mentioned that I'd like to have access to my file, now that my birth mother is dead. He said that I cannot have access to it, that the information in that file died with her. That's what the law states. However, he also said that the social worker could try, on my behalf, to get information from the death certificate, information including her next of kin. She could follow up any leads that might come out of that, and even act as a mediator between me and the next of kin. That would be fantastic! I will suggest this to Mary once she receives the certificate.*

Chapter 12

The Death Certificate arrived today, the 12th of October. This certificate states the cause of death and identifies the next of kin.

The day after I wrote this in my diary, Mary phoned, to let me know what else it contained. It stated that my birth mother died of lung cancer and secondaries. It also stated that she died before 1998: she had been only middle-aged. There was also another family member's name on the certificate. I asked Mary for the name and – you will never guess what she said. Yes, you got it: "I'm not at liberty to say" – even though my birth mother is deceased. It was at this point that I mentioned what my friend had told me. Despite this, Mary still wasn't willing to share any information with me.

She then proceeded to urge me to make an appointment with my GP, to discuss Margaret's cause of death. I agreed to do this, even though I knew that lung cancer is not hereditary. So, I didn't need to worry.

The next day, the 13th of October, I received another email from Mary asking me for my GP's phone number. She told me that she needed to speak to him directly. She also stressed that I needed to make an appointment to see him so that he could go through my mother's cause of death with me.

By this point I was starting to feel anxious. I asked her if there was anything else on the medical records that I should know about. She said, no, there wasn't. I felt as sure as anyone could be that lung cancer was not genetic. What was she keeping from me? I was in a panic all day as a result of her methods of communication. As I wrote in my diary: *Mary needs to take a deep breath and to think hard about how she converses with me. Doesn't she realise the unnecessary stress and panic she's causing?*

I managed to get an appointment with my GP. He was great. Panic over. He informed me there is nothing to worry about as regards lung cancer, as it is not hereditary. Deep down I had known that, but at least he had restored my peace of mind. Mary had put me through all the anxiety for nothing! Honestly, I feel that these social workers don't stop to think about the effect their actions might have on others, i.e. their clients. They need to learn to think before they act!

Mary phoned later that week to say she had been in touch with the secretary in Kilaloe, and that she had received confirmation that the information I'd relayed back to her, some 18 months ago, was in fact correct. (So, why put me through all that self-doubt over those months?) I leave it to you to determine.

Chapter 13

Once the death certificate had been submitted, I could request a formal copy of my birth certificate from the Adoption Authority. I needed Mary to write a report requesting its release.

Below is an extract from an email sent to me from Mary, asking me to write a letter to the Adoption Authority in Dublin explaining my reasons for wanting my original birth certificate.

10/20/15 at 2:19 PM

Dear Alice,

Currently I am in the process of requesting the release of your original birth certificate from the Adoption Authority of Ireland who ultimately can only make the decision to release this. To support my application, it would be beneficial if you also could write directly to the Adoption Authority stating your reasons for its release at this address: The Adoption Authority of Ireland, Shelbourne House, Shelbourne Road, Ballsbridge, Dublin 4.

Given the information available to me I am confident the lady I found appears to be your birth mother. Obviously, we are unable to confirm this as she is no longer alive R.I.P.

She further spelled out that, in this letter, I needed to put down:

The reasons why I wanted the birth certificate

What purpose I might have in wishing to obtain it

Finally, what I intended to do with any information contained in it

As I wrote in my diary: So, there we have it! She feels she's found the right person but, interestingly, is offering no guarantees. The first thing I'm asking myself is: shouldn't I be entitled to a guarantee? After all if the paper trail points to this person why the hesitancy to guarantee?

I felt utterly torn. I should have felt excited. But the reason why I wasn't jumping for joy was that I felt, in my gut, that the search was flawed. There were too many questions that seemed to have been brushed aside – for example, the date of birth of this woman. And then: why were they still following this lead when they had drawn a blank on it, and abandoned the search, back in April 2015? And why would this woman have travelled to Ireland from the UK to have her baby, to a place where she could have been recognised and might have been humiliated?

But what alternative did I have? I had only two: to go with the flow and to follow the next steps, or to refuse to play the game. As the latter would almost certainly have led Mary to cease the search altogether, I supposed that I was going to have to humour them.

Remember: the adoption authority would only release the birth certificate on a balance of rights basis for the birth mother. Here's a copy of the letter I sent to the Adoption Authority requesting the release of my birth certificate.

21st October 2015

Dear Carol,

In response to your request for clarification on my motives for seeking my birth certificate, the contents in the following paragraph should be used with my application.

My reason for seeking access to my birth certificate is twofold.

Firstly, I wish to fill in the gaps in my knowledge of my birth parents' backgrounds, allowing me to know my true identity. And, secondly, I wish to use the information as a basis to seek an insight into any genetic medical conditions that I might have inherited, whether that is obtained via records on file with the adoption agency or via her death certificate.

Can I stress again, I have no desire to use the information to seek a meeting with my birth parents' families. However, in order to gain the information, I seek regarding my birth parents' backgrounds, I would request that the relevant authorities contact these individuals on my behalf.

I found this to be one of the most frustrating periods in the entire search. I'd have thought it was obvious why I wanted this information, yet TUSLA and the Adoption Authority continually put obstacles in my way. They seemed determined to make it difficult for me to obtain what was rightfully mine. I suspected that the government agencies believed that, if they make it difficult enough for us adoptees to get the information we craved, we'd just give up on our searches. (No chance!)

Ironically, the adoption authority could still have refused to give me the certificate, even though my birth mother was deceased. They had to assess the circumstances around my case and then to decide (it is the law but is it right?) Personally, I felt that I should automatically get my birth certificate, especially since my birth mother was dead. This piece of paper was mine. It was my identity, and my possession of it could not affect anyone else.

A few days had passed since my last telephone conversation with Mary. I was doing a lot of thinking and enduring sleepless nights. My mind was constantly in overdrive, mulling over recent events.

I spoke to Mary's team leader again, as I was not entirely convinced that they had found the right person. I had a strong gut feeling about this. I expressed my reservations and was told that the team leader was certain they had the right person. So, now it was a guarantee – but that wasn't what Mary had said. She had even told me that they would stop the search if "that was the way I felt". In other words, I had to agree with whatever I was told. I was not allowed to have my own opinions about my case. ('Co-operate – or else you're on your own' was the message.)

Could she have done that? I supposed she could. At any rate, I told her to carry on, as long as she was sure that she had found the right woman. But, inside, I still wasn't convinced. I couldn't explain it. It was just a feeling.

This woman's age was incorrect, according to the non-identifying information I had gathered. Yet I knew that the women in such cases often gave false information, as they were terrified of being found out. Even so, this woman's age was completely off. Also, her social circumstances at the time of the pregnancy did not feel right.

I had to keep reminding myself that Mary was only giving me scenarios, not facts, surrounding my birth mother's circumstances. And that, at the end of the day, I was supposed to believe everything they told me to be true – even though, deep down, I felt that it might not be.

Chapter 14

I spoke to Mary, who informed me that the report had been sent off to the Adoption Authority. It could take a few weeks for it to be assessed.

While waiting for the birth certificate to be released I'd been thinking about the next of kin mentioned on the death certificate. I wanted to try and trace this person. He or she could potentially be a full or a half-sibling and might be able to give me some information regarding my birth mother, her life, the circumstances surrounding my adoption, medical information, extended family, where she was buried, etc.

I had spoken to a friend of mine, someone quite knowledgeable in this area. He advised that I could start searching, with my social worker acting as a mediator, once the next of kin was found. I mentioned this to Mary and offered to write a letter to this person explaining what I was looking for.

I was told "No, not at this point in time". And my immediate feeling was: *here we go again.* Personally, I did not understand why we couldn't. This was yet another of those occasions where Mary was dragging her feet and dealing with each issue individually, rather than multitasking. In my opinion she was just wasting time, just as she had done from June 2014 to April 2015.

Chapter 15

As I wrote in my diary:

I haven't heard anything back regarding the report and my birth certificate.

So today I decided to phone the Adoption Authority myself to see if they had received the report and made a decision. I'm fed-up with waiting. As you have probably gathered, I'm not the most patient person in the world!

I spoke to a lovely lady. She said, 'They have received the report but have not, as yet, made a decision.' When I mentioned my name, she knew who I was and asked me to phone back the following week for an update. I felt a little better after that conversation because at least I knew that someone is looking at my case.

And later*: I received a phone call today, the 9th of December, from that lovely lady in the Adoption Authority to tell me my birth certificate has been released. She's posting it out to me this afternoon. Fantastic news!*

Finally, on the 14th of December I received an official copy of my birth certificate. It was practically the same as the one I had located in the General Register Office, back in June 2014. There was only one-real difference: it was on official paper. Strangely enough, I felt really happy about this, simply because no one could put doubts in my head anymore. Although I still had a niggling feeling that we were trying to trace the wrong person. (We had the right name but because it's such a common name that I remained worried.)

Once I had received my birth certificate, I had some questions for Mary.

Now that I had the actual birth certificate in hand, could any more information be released from my file?

Could the burial details of my birth mother be released, for example?

Could Mary at this point make contact with the next of kin, in order to progress answers to the background questions already submitted back in November 2015?

Mary responded: "Are you by any chance visiting Ireland over the holidays? Prior to moving to the next stage, I feel it would be helpful if we could sit down face-to-face, so that I could discuss the options open to you."

I puzzled over this – even agonised over it. What did she mean by 'options open to me?' Did she have some new developments to discuss that she would prefer not to discuss over the phone?

I found this infuriating. She always managed to put ideas in my head, where I started thinking all sorts of things. It really wasn't fair on me to be first dangling a carrot and then making me wait a few weeks before telling me anything concrete. It felt cruel. Sometimes I thought it was enough to drive me insane.

Now bear in mind, I lived in England and we were then on the run-up to Christmas, the most expensive time of the year. On December 15th, I replied by email, "Unfortunately, we are not coming to Ireland over Christmas and New Year, as Alex is revising for his GCSE mock exams in January. Can we discuss moving forward via Skype, email or instant messaging instead?" I also left two voicemail messages asking her to phone me.

The next day I started worrying and panicking over what information she might have found that she wasn't sharing with me. I felt in limbo, wondering at her urgency regarding meeting me face to face, especially at Christmastime.

Later that day I decided to email again, this time copying in the team leader.

12/16/15 at 1:11 PM

Mary,

I need to express my feelings to you over the recent communication from your department.

On Monday I received an email suggesting that I need to meet in person with you. I have responded by email and left voicemails but have yet to hear back from you.

I must convey I am both concerned and annoyed by this turn of events. Meeting personally has never been an issue before so, what has changed? Your lack of response since the email on Monday has raised an awful lot of scenarios in my mind and these have been left festering now for 48 hours.

You need to see this from my situation and recognise that if you remain silent for this length of time immediately after bringing a new scenario into our dealings, then you are causing unnecessary distress in an already lengthy saga. I am mentally and emotionally capable of handling this whole process and have accepted time delays in the past as par for the course. But what I do find extremely frustrating is a lack of ongoing communication in a timely manner, especially when the conversation has been started from your office.

I have suggested alternatives to a meeting as we have no plans to travel home to Ireland and I would politely request that you respond to this email, in order to put my mind at ease.

This is the reply:

12/16/15 at 2:15 PM

Hi,

Thank you for your e-mail and I note your concerns. In my last email to you I gave you my available times and invited you to meet with me. I am available to take a phone call from you at 10-10.30 am on Tuesday 23rd December. I don't generally give appointments like this but in response to your levels of distress I feel on this occasion that it is appropriate. I look forward to hearing from you.

With best regards

Mary

Levels of distress, indeed!

The original email had not invited me to any telephone conversation on the 23rd: it had only given dates to meet in person. As I wrote that night: *No wonder I'm distressed. . . I think I'm going to need counselling for the distress caused by their inability to communicate and understand what adoptees go through when searching for birth parents!*

On the 17th of December I was so upset with the events of the previous days that Max phoned Mary's team leader to complain about the way I had been treated. He asked that the social worker please make time to respond to my emails. (Let's see how long that will last!)

The team leader told him that Mary was hitting a brick wall in locating the next of kin mentioned on the death certificate. She also said that Mary was unsure if the next of kin was blood-related. If the person were not blood-related it was unclear legally if they could give burial details. In any case, TUSLA will only look into this if the person is found.

The reason the team leader wanted me to go to Ireland at Christmas, the most inconvenient and expensive time of the year, was simply to discuss the next step in the search. There wasn't anything new on file. Mary didn't have any new developments for me. She just wanted to meet me, to tick another box. Words failed me when I learned this. Mary had put me through all this anxiety completely unnecessarily.

By this point I was seriously considering seeking legal advice. I felt that there wasn't any compassion from the social services. This was just a box-ticking exercise for them. They did not consider the effects, mental and emotional, that an undertaking like this has on an individual.

As I wrote that night: *So, as we are 18 months into the search I'd like to touch on how this period of my life is affecting me so far.*

Mentally, it's been tough for me. My advice to anyone thinking about starting a search is, make sure you have a good network of family and friends around you. It's very important to have their support because you don't know when you will have a hurdle to jump over or a high wall to climb. You may get some doors slammed in your face. You will need to be thick-skinned and strong. I have been very lucky because I have my husband, my 15-year-old son, my sister, my mum and some very good friends to get me through this chapter in my life. I also have my running. Since my search began, I ran a couple of 10k's, 3 half-marathons and I hope to run a marathon early next year. It has helped me to have my running to focus on. It was and is a great stress reliever!

Chapter 16

The 23rd of December 2015 finally arrived. This was the day of my telephone conversation with Mary.

I went to the gym first thing as I felt I needed a little stress relief. I phoned Mary from my bedroom and spent 50 minutes on the phone. I was alone. You need to remember that this is the 23rd of December, two days before Christmas.

She had some shocking news for me, starting with, "Are you sitting down?"

Then she told me that, just two days before she issued her report to the Adoption Authority she had discovered that I had an adopted sibling. Oh, my God! My instant reaction was *why had it taken her so long to tell me?* She submitted that report back in October, two long months ago. Why hadn't she told me a couple of weeks ago when she had asked me if I was going home to Ireland for Christmas? Why put me through all that stress and anxiety – and then not tell me? And why on earth had she and the team leader denied then that they had any new information for me?

While I was speechless, she informed me that my sibling is male and had been born after me. *I have a brother, or maybe a half-brother.* Mary was currently contacting the child and family agencies in Ireland as there might even have been more adopted siblings born in Ireland. If Mary could locate this person she asked if I was prepared to do a DNA test. I said I was.

I felt a little confused because I had thought my birth mother lived in the UK. . . It looks like she got pregnant twice and seemed to have travelled back to Ireland on both occasions, to give birth as well as to put them up for adoption. This doesn't somehow ring true to me.

As I wrote: *This feels very weird, almost surreal. I am both happy and excited with this news. I am also very emotional. The tears are still streaming down my face as I try to comprehend the fact that I have a brother and that he may be able to fill in some gaps for me as regards my history. Though I am also very wary that Mary may not have found the right person.*

I felt almost afraid to be too excited, as if it all might be snatched away from me again!

I had been told the death certificate had been issued in the UK. There was the name and address of the next of kin on it, but Mary was unsure if he was blood-related, possibly only a friend of the family. She was going to follow this up in the new year. Mary had asked if I was still thinking about going to Ireland in the new year. I had told her I would look into flights, but it would have to be February, after Alex's GCSE mock exams.

I had been reading a book, about the exporting of illegitimate Irish children to America in the 1950s and 1960s. These babies were taken from their mothers in the mother and baby homes and shipped to America because the Americans wanted to adopt white babies instead of the black ones more readily available. The Catholic Church in Ireland didn't want these Catholic babies to be brought up in Irish Protestant families: instead, they exported the babies to America. The nuns even gained financially from this baby export business. In my opinion this book is a "must-read" but it should also carry a health warning, as it will make your blood boil! Both Sean Ross Abbey (where I was born) and Stamullen (where I was adopted from) feature in the book. Babies were exported to America from both these institutions – at a price.

And the Church was less than helpful, even to me. When I was 18 or 19, I had first tried to look for my birth mother, but I'd had, so to speak, the door slammed in my face. I had gone to see Father Reagan, the parish priest for Stamullen at the time, and told him I was trying to trace my birth mother. He had dismissed me almost instantly, telling me to be grateful for what I had. That meeting had lasted all of five minutes! (When I finished reading this book, I was shocked to learn that Father Reagan had actually been involved in the exporting of babies from Stamullen and other places.)

Also, I suddenly feared that my adoptive father may have given "donations" to the priest before being allowed to adopt me.

I asked Mary to check this out and she confirmed that there was nothing on my record to suggest that he had given monetary donations – though this doesn't mean much, as many records for that period had been destroyed.

As I wrote in my diary: *I wouldn't hold it against my dad if he had made donations, because I know he truly believed the babies would have benefited, which we did. But, somehow, I would like to know.*

Perhaps I am just the kind of person who likes to know.

Chapter 17

Christmas had been and gone. I'd deliberately not thought about my search. I had longed to have a nice, stress-free Christmas with family and friends.

However, I did manage to book flights to Ireland from the 2nd to the 4th of February. I was supposed to meet Mary for the first time on the 3rd, at 10.30 a.m. She seemed very keen to meet me face-to-face. I assumed, or perhaps only hoped, she had some new information for me. However, I did not know for sure.

Since December there had already been another major development. I'd recently learned that my birth mother had given birth to another baby and had also given him away.

(Yes, I have another brother!)

I wasn't sure if both brothers are full siblings or half-siblings, so I asked Mary to double check that the signatures on all the consent forms looked identical. She told me that they did. This suggests that this woman had given birth to three children but had given us all away.

So many complicated feelings!

As I wrote:

I had a strange thought today after I spoke to the social worker. I was telling Max the latest updates and he suddenly said, "You may be a twin!" It's not impossible: after all, I was born eight weeks early and weighed only 4 lbs and 4 oz. So, I phoned Mary and she said, "No you're definitely not a twin." It is recorded that this woman only gave birth to one baby, a girl, on April 20th, 1969. Mary is not at liberty to say where the other two babies were born. However, she did mention they were born after me, on different dates and in different years.

Wow, this is a lot to take in! I have two younger siblings. This is presumably why Mary feels she needed to speak to me face-to-face, though I still feel it's wrong to keep any information from me especially, when she knows how anxious I am to find out the truth about myself.

I had to admit to myself that I was still struggling with the concept that this woman, allegedly my birth mother, and certainly living in the UK, got pregnant three times and each time travelled back to Ireland to give them away. Why not simply give them up for adoption in the UK? Why run the risk of someone's finding out your secrets by going back to Ireland? It just didn't seem logical, but I sensed that I may be getting closer. As I wrote: *It's going to be an interesting meeting!* It was.

Chapter 18

As I scribbled on a momentous day: *It is the morning of the 2nd of February 2016.*

I flew to Ireland today. I am staying with my mum and my sister is taking me to the meeting tomorrow. I wonder if this meeting will be a box-ticking exercise or will I receive new information!

To recap on the developments so far: in April 2015, Mary informed me that she had hit a brick wall and was starting the search afresh. She was tracking a woman in the UK. This woman was deceased, but the teams of social workers believed her to have been my birth mother. I had expressed reservations: this woman was younger than the age given on my non-identifying information about my mother; she had also given birth thrice and had given all three babies away. She had died in the UK and there was a next of kin listed on the death certificate, who might or might not be blood related. This was where we had got to.

You can imagine the scenarios my mum, my sister and I were coming up with in car on the way to the meeting! My sister agreed with my instinct, that they hadn't found the right person – but who could tell what new evidence the meeting might produce?

My sister dropped me off outside a very old, run-down building, and drove on with my mum to the shopping centre. I was to phone them when I was finished.

I walked through the door to the main reception and asked for Mary. When I mentioned my name to the receptionist, she looked curiously at me, as if putting a face to the name. Maybe I had a reputation of being a nag, seeing as I did phone a lot, chasing information. *Well, I needed to,* I thought, *or else they would have given up months ago!* I needed to keep them on their toes.

I was asked to wait in the waiting room: Mary would be with me shortly. She didn't keep me waiting long. She appeared very pleasant, and, I thought, seemed genuinely glad to meet me. Mary escorted me to another floor, to what looked like a boardroom, though very dated, almost 70s. She then sat opposite me with a very thick blue file. I longed to grab hold of it. That file held the information for which I had been searching for my whole life! I had this desperate urge to grab the file and run but I restrained myself.

It was an exceptionally long and interesting meeting.

As I wrote later:

Where do I start...? Mary started off by telling me the non-identifying information I had was correct. (So, does this mean that my birth mother's age on the non-identifying information is correct?) My birth mother was admitted to Sean Ross Abbey the same day she went into labour. She was admitted as a private patient, meaning that £100 was paid to the nuns.

Let me explain about the £100. When a woman was admitted to Sean Ross Abbey in the 40s, 50s and 60s they had the option of going in as a private patient. This meant they paid £100 so they could leave after the baby was adopted. If the money wasn't paid to the Abbey, they were obliged to stay and work in the laundry or kitchen or similar to work off their debt of £100. Being a private patient meant my birth mother didn't have to do the heavy-duty chores like the less advantaged women. (We still aren't sure how she paid this, as her occupation was listed as factory worker. Mary seems to think she might have paid this money by using her stamps.)

It appears she stayed with me and breastfed me until the 13th of May, although this is not certain as Mary said wet nurses were often used in these institutions. I don't want to think about that. I want to believe she stayed with me until the day she gave me away. According to Mary my birth mother transported me herself to Stamullen.

I am not sure how she did this. This is such a lot to take in!

Mary still believes my birth mother died in 1997 or 1998. She is not at liberty to say when. She died aged 50 or 51 years and is buried in the UK. She is not at liberty to say where.

I still cannot believe that this woman is my birth mother. She must have been an extraordinarily strong woman to have had three babies, travel to Ireland from the UK to have them and give them all up for adoption, but. . . But how can a woman have a premature baby, breastfeed her for three weeks and then transport the baby herself, personally, to Stamullen to give her up? The thing is, she didn't do this only once: she did it three times! Did she really endure this ordeal three times and then return to the UK – just as if nothing had happened? This just does not feel right. My gut feeling is stronger than ever – that this is the wrong person – but Mary is convinced she is right.

My birth mother, to assume that Mary was right, was an only child with a secondary school education. Back in the early 60s secondary school education was free up until the age of fourteen, after which it was fee-paying. We couldn't be sure she achieved any qualifications, as her occupation was a factory worker. She probably hadn't, because, back then, young girls with secondary school qualifications generally went to work in the civil service.

In the meeting Mary also told me that she had been searching for the next of kin, the named informant on the death certificate. She confirmed that this man was my brother and was living in the UK – not a friend of the family, as originally suggested. So, this revelation meant that I had potentially yet another brother or half-brother. *(OMG, how many babies did this woman have? I thought.)* I was struggling to get my head around this.

It appeared I had three brothers. Two that my birth mother gave away and one she kept.

Mary had two general locations for this last brother and had already been in contact with the DHSS in the UK – who refused to disclose any information because of the Data Protection Act. Which seemed fair enough: I wouldn't wish my own private information being given out. It was frustrating, though. Every time that I felt I might be getting somewhere ended with my taking a few steps back. . . On the other hand, Mary said she would contact the Salvation Army to see if they might have an address for him.

He was not given up for adoption. My birth mother had four babies and kept one of the four. Why?

As I wrote later: *It is believed she had me and gave me up. She then had another baby and kept that one. She had two more and gave them both away. Not sure if that is the right order – I need to check this out. OMG, how could this woman have four children and keep only one? It does not make any sense. It appears that when she gave me away and fell pregnant the second time, she kept her second child. Mary did say that sometimes, when a woman gave away a baby, she becomes pregnant again straightaway, to fill in the void of losing her baby.*

I have been going through scenarios in my head. Maybe she couldn't afford to keep the other two babies? Perhaps she was put under pressure not to keep them? Perhaps she found it so hard leaving me behind she couldn't face that again? Maybe she feared for a baby's well-being where she was living? – but then, she kept one. It is mind-blowing. I can't get my head around it.

Mary and I took a break after 90 minutes. I didn't know what I was feeling – it was all confusion – except that I was extremely excited to learn that I might possibly have three siblings. I phoned Max, back in the UK, as I was about to burst. I also phoned my sister, who was waiting for me. Lots to talk about, all round.

At the end of the two-and-a-half-hour meeting Mary again asked me to confirm that I was prepared to do a DNA test, to be assured that this man really is my brother and also, of course, to ensure that they had found the correct birth mother. I said I would.

I agreed to it, mainly, to rule them out, though. I longed for three brothers! – but then, the woman herself was dead. . .

I was asked to contact the Adoption Services in the UK, mainly so I could have counselling if I needed it. I'd said all along that I neither needed nor wanted counselling. However, if I contacted them, they might possibly be able to locate my potential siblings, as the adoption laws are different in the UK. (I later managed to contact an Adoption Agency, who said that they could try and locate my sibling living in the UK, upon payment of a fee.)

When I asked Mary to start searching for the other two siblings given up for adoption, I was told, "One step at a time. We'll try and find the sibling in the UK first." This is intensely frustrating. I could not see why we couldn't have had a couple of searches going on alongside each other.

According to the social worker, of the two babies given up for adoption, one had been born in Sean Ross Abbey, while the other was a private adoption. My birth mother had been caring for her elderly mother when she placed the third baby for adoption. Mary told me that the third baby had been born in St Gerard's hospital in Limerick. I was unconvinced about this information, though, as I couldn't find a St Gerard's hospital in Limerick. I worried that Mary was getting her facts mixed.

Neither adopted brother have initiated a search for any siblings. There was nothing on file, at any rate.

Mary also assured me she was going to try and find out my birth mother's burial place.

At the very end of the meeting I mentioned to Mary that I had a strange feeling that my birth mother had been taken advantage of, or even abused. I could not get this feeling out of my head, even though it might not be true and was certainly illogical. It was just an intuition I had.

Two and a half hours later the meeting had ended. I met my mum and sister, utterly exhausted, with a mind rushing at ninety miles an hour. I was going over and over the past two and a half hours in my head while trying to scribble down notes in my diary. I phoned Max again whilst on our way to the restaurant and told him my news. It was very surreal. The new developments suddenly didn't feel real to me. My mum, sister and I arrived at the restaurant, where we dissected the whole meeting intensely and in detail, coming up with various possibilities and trying to make these new developments believable.

We particularly considered the story about "Margaret" having birthed four babies and given away three. It just did not feel right that a woman could do this – unless she had kept the youngest because she had remained with his father. We couldn't understand how she kept getting pregnant while living in the UK – where birth control was possible – but continued travelling back to Ireland to have the babies and to give them up for adoption. Surely by travelling back to Ireland she was running the risk of discovery? Why not give up the babies for adoption in the UK, where there was no such stigma?

This woman – my birth mother, possibly – had died in the UK, at a young age, of lung cancer. Had she been alone? Married? Had she lived a rough life? I sensed that she had endured a lot. She might have been abused. She might have been very naive when it came to sex.

I spent a couple of days with my mum before travelling back to the UK on the 4th of February. I felt almost as if I had had some out-of-body experience. None of this felt real. I returned to the UK, still trying to get my head around everything.

The day after I got back, I phoned a friend of mine who knows a great deal about adoption in Ireland. I told him about the new developments, and he was very pleased for me. He confirmed that it was common back in the 1960s for women to have a few babies. As Mary had suggested, they were sometimes so devastated and overwhelmed by their loss they became pregnant a second time to fill the hole in their lives. You see, in Catholic Ireland in the 1960s contraception was unknown, and sex education in schools unheard-of. When young girls fell pregnant out of wedlock they were almost universally condemned, both by the church and by society, and considered solely to blame for their sinful act. Men, on the other hand, got away with acting on impulse. They were almost never held responsible, whereas women had to be church-abiding citizens. The shame was brought upon the women and their families; the men just walked away, carrying on with their lives as before.

Unmarried mothers (along with their children) were also treated as second-class citizens. When these women went into the laundries, or into mother and baby homes, they were made to work, often in vile conditions, as recompense for their sins. They were often abused physically, as well as mentally. If only these young women – sometimes just girls – had been educated, and if only contraception had been made available to them, what pain and heartache would have been spared – and if only Ireland could just come out of the Dark Ages and step into the 21st century, innocent men and women could have access to their files, their identity and their history!

My friend also suggested that I get in touch with the Adoption Authority in Dublin to see if there were any matches on the Contact Register, just to see if either of the two adopted siblings might have initiated a search there.

I did this but, sadly, there weren't any matches.

Chapter 19

It is the 26th of February 2016.

I am at home watching the award-winning film Philomena for the third time. It feels more heart breaking each time I watch it. I have an ever-increasing hunger to know what happened to my birth mother. I need to know the circumstances surrounding my conception – and my birth – in that awful institution. As I look at this film and see how the women were treated, I have a desperate hunger to discover my history and to locate my siblings. I also need to know what happened to my mother, what kind of a life she endured.

I have decided to try and track down the nuns that were in Stamullen in 1969. I feel I need to do something to try to speed things up.

Now I remembered that, when I was little, Mum and Dad used to take my sister, my brother and me to Stamullen, not only to see the babies but also to visit the nuns. I remember clearly walking through the main doorway and into a reception area. The door on the left led to where the babies stayed, in old iron cots set out in rows. The babies were either asleep, sitting up or trying to climb out. I remember feeling sad for these babies. They had no proper parents. No loving, warm, cosy home.

The room on the right was the Mother Superior's office, Sister Barbara. The Mother Superior when I had been adopted was apparently Sister Aloysius. I clearly remember walking through the building: it was very clinical, rather like a hospital. There was another room, where older children were playing. These children looked sad to me. I remember *thinking I could have been one of them. I was one of the lucky ones.*

We used to take tins of biscuits for the kiddies and the staff. When I was in 5th year at school, I was part of an enterprising project when our year-group set up a company to make and sell draught excluders. The idea behind the project was to understand how to set up and run a small business. We did this for a year, and, at the end we wound up the company and made a profit. We donated the profit, of £200, to Stamullen. A couple of other girls came with me, to present the cheque to Sister Pauline. (Though my favourite nun had been Sister Marie Louise; I still remember her.)

So, all these memories got me thinking again and I phoned my sister in Ireland. She seemed to think the St Clare nuns were in a home in Dublin. I phoned the home in hopes of reconnecting with Sister Marie Louise but was told that she had passed away four years before. I spoke to Sister Marie, who was very pleasant: she asked me to put everything in writing and promised to get back to me. So, I immediately wrote back, sharing all the details I possessed about myself and my parents and also the information I'd been allowed to know about "Margaret". Sister Marie wrote back, regretting that she did not have any additional information for me.

Still, it had been worth a try.

Chapter 20

In March 2016 I wrote:

Today, I made some phone calls and managed to find an Adoption Agency in Manchester willing to possibly locate my UK-based sibling. (This is a private agency, so there would be a fee attached.) I explained that I wanted to find my sibling, but I didn't have much information, as identifying information regarding my birth mother is not allowed under Irish law.

I also told the lady at the agency that she would need to liaise with my social worker in Ireland and would also be obliged to sign an agreement stating that she wouldn't pass on any identifying information to me. (This is all so very frustrating. We are in the 21st century, my birth mother is dead, and I'm still not allowed information regarding my own sibling!)

Anyway, the agency agreed to take on my case. All I need now is for Mary to get in contact with them and start the ball rolling. Though Mary has yet to receive the birth certificate for the UK sibling. Maybe the adoption agency will have more success!

I emailed Mary that same day, to see if she had any updates for me – any new information on my half-sibling living in the UK. This is the baby boy Margaret kept and also the next of kin named on her death certificate. I say "half-sibling" because Mary referred to him in that way. Below is an extract from the email she sent me:

Mar 7 at 4:40 PM

In the meantime, I am still searching for your half-sibling but with no success. I contacted an agency your birth mother was linked to, within the last few days, about which I am not at liberty to disclose information. This agency had a telephone number for one of your birth mother's relatives. I spoke with a lady from this agency this morning, after which she called this number but only got a disconnected tone. She advised me that this relative had lived at the address I recently wrote to, and from which I have had no response. It now seems apparent that this person is no longer living at this address.

I also received information that your birth mother gave birth to another son, one not to my knowledge placed for adoption, who was born before you and the other child she kept. I am in the process of trying to locate this person and today wrote to DHSS UK requesting if they could confirm if he is alive or deceased. I will let you know as soon as I have more information. I appreciate that this is yet more difficult information for you to process. I will be happy to chat with you about this if you call.

Well, there it was: The plot continued to thicken. Let me briefly recap.

According to Mary, my birth mother gave birth to five children and gave three of them away. Apparently, she had a baby boy before me. This meant that she could have only been seventeen or eighteen when she gave birth to her first boy, perhaps even younger. She kept this baby.

Then she had me when she was 20. She travelled to Ireland to give birth, in Sean Ross Abbey. She stayed with me for three weeks and transported me personally to the Stamullen Mother and Baby Home, where I was adopted. She later became pregnant for a third and a fourth time, and had two more baby boys, who were also given up for adoption, in Ireland. This poor woman then fell pregnant a fifth time. She had another baby boy, which she kept, returning with him to the UK. Therefore, I could have four siblings.

As I wrote: *I am really struggling to get my head around all this, especially as I have never been completely confident that the social workers have found the right person. She may have the same name as my birth mother, but I am not convinced that she is my birth mother. Something just doesn't feel right. I worry that they have two women with the same name and have mixed up their stories – or that Mary has blended them into one. I really doubt that Mary has read through my file properly. I sense that she is pulling information from various directions. It has got to the point now where none of it makes any sense. You can imagine the confusion I feel. I have loads of questions:*

How could my birth mother have been able to afford to keep and care for the first baby while still in her teens?

How could she have three more babies, travel to Ireland each time, and give them up for adoption?

Who took care of the baby boy born before me when she travelled to Ireland?

How could she manage to keep the eldest and youngest babies?

My imagination was working overtime. Had my birth mother been abused? Had she been sleeping around? Had she suffered mental health issues? She may perhaps have been in several different relationships. . . I had to keep reminding myself that all this happened in the 60s and 70s. But she wasn't living in Catholic Ireland, so why travel back there on three separate occasions to have her babies? Why deliberately choose to return to a place where you knew you would be judged and ill-treated for getting pregnant outside of wedlock?

Ireland, back in the 60s, was a place where there was no such thing as contraception or sex education. Of course, Margaret had also been an only child and might not have had anyone to confide in. Also, at least during her first pregnancy, she might not have understood exactly what was going on with her body.

The more I wondered, the more determined I felt to find out my birth mother's social circumstances during this time. Mary had informed me that she has tried to get information from the DHSS in the UK but without success, because of the Data Protection Act. She had also been in touch with the agency my birth mother was linked to before she died. This agency, I believe, was the hospice where she eventually died of lung cancer. Of course, Mary would not tell me where this agency was. This was all so frustrating!

Easter break was fast approaching when Mary would be on holiday for two-and-a-half weeks. So, nothing would happen during that time. I simply had to sit back and put all this to the back of my mind. (Easier said than done!)

Chapter 21

It is the 12th of April and Mary is back from her holiday. I emailed her asking her for any updates and the reply was that she had received the birth certificates for both siblings: the youngest and the eldest. She is still looking for their addresses. I suppose that's something. Having their names and place of birth should make it easier to locate them. She's still not giving me their names, though.

On April 19th Mary called me. She had been in contact with the adoption agency I commissioned to seek my younger siblings. Mary was willing to release these siblings' birth certificates, but only on the understanding that they did not pass on that information to me.

Meanwhile, the adoption agency believed that they could locate my siblings in the UK, given the information provided. They could do this at a fee: £350 to search for one sibling, and then an extra £100 to trace the second. I have discussed this with Max, and we have agreed to go ahead. I considered this to be a major development, given that I might finally learn about my birth mother and the history of my blood relatives. I desperately needed to fill in the gaps. I wanted to try to understand – the good and the bad – of what my birth mother had gone through, 47 years ago.

I had asked Mary again about my birth mother's choosing to keep only her eldest and her youngest baby. Confusingly, Mary was instead saying that she chose to keep the third baby, and not the fifth one. So, my birth mother kept the baby she had after me. How confusing for me – and how painful! Almost as bad, Mary generally seemed to forget whatever she had told me last. She previously wrote that the eldest and youngest babies stayed with the birth mother. The emails below certainly suggest this:

Apr 18 at 4:47 PM

Hi Mary,

The Certificates you received: are they for the 2 siblings that she kept? The eldest and younger male?

Alice

Apr 18 at 5:02 PM

Yes, Alice. they are for the siblings she kept. They are the eldest and youngest males she kept.

As I wrote, later and privately, in my diary:

I feel as if Mary is playing mind games with me and I am struggling with this whole scenario as it is. I don't really need this confusion. This is a typical example of her getting details muddled up. Good job I am keeping my diaries. . . I need Mary to be consistent. I also need to be sure I can trust her.

So, now it appears that this woman kept the first and third baby and gave away her other three. What kind of a life did this woman have? She must have been a strong woman to be able to give birth to five babies and to only keep two of them. I just cannot get my head around this at all.

It suddenly hit me that it had been a year since, in April 2015, Mary told me that she had hit a brick wall and needed to start the search for my birth mother from scratch. Mary then decided to go back and follow up a lead on a woman she had already ruled out at least once. This woman, Margaret, was now deceased but had lived in the UK. My understanding was she was born in Ireland and moved to the UK in her late teens.

Margaret had, it appeared, five children, of which she kept two and gave away three. (At first, I was told only about the two other babies she gave away – I only recently found out about the two whom she kept. I found out about the first in February and the second in March.)

As I wrote: *So, one of these days, I might meet one of my brothers. It's not entirely impossible.*

Chapter 22

On the 20th of April, my 47th birthday, I spoke to the lady at the Adoption and Tracing Agency in Manchester, who agreed to take on my case. I admitted that I didn't have a lot of information for her, due to the Irish legal system. She would also have to communicate directly with my social worker in Ireland. I also told her that Mary had already accessed the birth certificates for the two of my potential siblings who were based in the UK. She promised to liaise with Mary and get back to me. I put down the phone with a rush of optimism, feeling that at last I was making progress.

After that phone call I had a call from another social worker, one based in Dublin, with the Adoption Authority. (I thought: *it's all happening today!*) This social worker, Ben, was phoning me in relation to a match that had arisen on the Contact Register.

The National Adoption Contact Preference Register was a register that I'd signed up to back in 2014, when I'd first started my search. If a sibling (or a birth parent, for instance) had already registered it flags up a match. Well, Ben informed me that there was a match.

Wow, my youngest brother wanted to make contact!

I was told that he had been born in 1975. Ben had sent a letter to him in November 2015 but had not received a response, nor to the letters he has sent since. So, he might not still be living at the address he had given (or even still be living in Ireland).

I wanted to know why it had taken so long for Ben to phone me and let me know there had been a match. Five months! Still, I always find that everything goes at snail's pace. I was asked if I would be interested in meeting a potential relative. I said yes, of course I would. Ben was going to write another letter, six weeks after sending the first, to the address he had. (Hopefully, he would get a reply.)

And here is yet another example of where Mary, the social worker, simply got mixed up. According to the social worker in the Adoption Authority, my birth mother gave up my youngest sibling: he was registered on the contact register in 2005 as an adopted person seeking contact with birth parents or siblings. My birth mother had not kept him, as previously suggested by Mary.

I asked Ben if he could see on the files any record of other siblings. One had been born after me, but still before the younger brother, the one seeking contact. Ben could only tell me that one of my brothers had been born in 1974, and that he – Ben – was perfectly willing to attempt to contact him but that he could only contact the brothers one at a time. This was possibly the most frustrating part of all: if only he had been willing to search for both brothers simultaneously it might have speeded things up – at least, a little.

Still, as I wrote that night; *What a day. I cannot believe that all this has happened on my 47th birthday! Have I finally got a breakthrough in my case?*

A few days later, I recorded that I had "just about got my head around" recent developments. Still, it remained a lot to take in. I was still struggling with the fact that my birth mother had given birth to five children, kept two and given away three. Also, despite her living in the UK from a young age, she had chosen to travel back to Ireland three times to have her babies, only to give them up for adoption.

Why? Why would she have returned to Ireland? Why would she have put herself through the embarrassment and humiliation of everyone finding her shame? – And, not just once, but three times. . .

I can't get these questions out of my head.

I emailed Mary today regarding my four siblings. Below are copies of the emails:

Apr 25 at 4:29 PM

Hi Mary,

Just had a thought. Is there any way of checking the signatures on the affidavits and the UK birth certificates to see if they match?

Alice

Apr 25 at 5:02 PM

Hi Alice,

I have checked this and neither of the signatures are Margaret's. I checked with my colleague re birth of the other child placed from Sean Ross. That child had a normal delivery and was a very healthy weight. There was no record of a premature birth. I will keep trying, Alice.

With best regards

Mary

Just to clarify, signatures for 1 and 3 do not match 2, 4 and 5. If this is the case surely, they are 2 different people?

Alice

Apr 25 at 5:10 PM

Can you give me a quick ring, Alice, please?

Well, I phoned Mary as requested, and – yes – I had a new, if unwelcome, development.

My worst suspicions seemed to be coming true.

It appeared that my alleged younger brother, "baby three", the baby Margaret kept, had been born in the UK in early November 1969. I had been born on April 20th, 1969, eight weeks early, and he had been born in November. *Six and a half months after me,* to be precise. Surely this must have been impossible?

My birth mother would have had to get pregnant straightaway after having me in order to give birth in early November 1969. And this also seemed unlikely, as she had stayed in Sean Ross Abbey for three weeks after giving birth. Mary, however, seemed to think it possible, because women back then were likely to get pregnant immediately after relinquishing a baby, in order to replace the child, they had lost.

My first question was: how could she get pregnant when she was in Sean Ross Abbey for three weeks immediately after my birth? (I should add that the women there were surrounded by nuns, and not permitted to leave the grounds.) Mary told me – wait for it – that there were groundsmen around the Abbey. If the women really wanted to get pregnant again, they would probably have had chances.

I was not at all sure that I liked where Mary was going with this. She seemed to be suggesting not only that my birth mother slept around to get pregnant, but also that "these women" had absolutely no self-respect. I hated the picture she was painting of the unfortunate women in these awful places. I thought *Mary is clutching at straws. I think, as I have thought for several months now, that she has simply got hold of the wrong person. I sense that she and her colleagues at TUSLA are looking for a quick end to this story. They are trying to convince me they have the correct person, just in order to save face.*

Secondly, even if the mother refused to give her own body a chance to recover from having a baby, how could a baby born at between 24 to 26 weeks have survived? Especially back in 1969. The facilities available almost certainly were not advanced enough to care for a premature baby of that age, not even in the UK!

I was convinced the social workers had got it all wrong. My best guess was that Mary had found two separate pieces of information for two women who happened to share the same name, confused the two pieces of information, and blended it into one person. I also sensed that she might be quite embarrassed about this and be desperately trying to convince herself that she is right, so that she didn't look foolish in front of me and her colleagues.

Now the woman who signed the three affidavits – for me, for the baby born in 1974 and for the baby born in 1975 – appeared to be the same person. The signatures are identical, even though she signed my admissions form with a long name and my consent form with a shortened version of the same name. (I believe that she was known by the shortened version of her name.) All three signatures on the affidavits match. This woman also gave the same address on the three affidavits.

The signatures on the birth certificates of the babies born in the UK were different – and I, *personally,* believed the babies were born to a *completely different woman.* I did *not* believe that these were my blood relatives. The social worker was suggesting that a friend may have signed the birth certificates. Unfortunately, there was no signature to compare it to. She was simply clutching at straws.

Mary had hinted that this woman, meaning the woman in the UK, had lived at the Irish address on file and then moved to the UK before I was born (supposedly, because she had given birth to the first baby in the UK). She had also hinted that the woman who signed the affidavits might have given a false name and address. Or that she may have been a friend or relative who had assumed the identity of the woman who moved to the UK, as this had been known to happen. Young women back then – those finding themselves pregnant out of wedlock – sometimes did whatever they could to hide their identities.

To clarify: we were talking about two separate women here, though they may have lived in the same area at one time. Mary's theory was that the woman who signed the affidavits had given a false name, i.e. had stolen the identity of another woman. If this was the case, she did very well to keep up the pretence for six years!

I did not believe this for a second. I knew, deep down, that my social worker and her colleagues had found the wrong woman. Mary needed to hold her hands up and admit that she had made a mistake.

As I wrote that night: *If I'm right, then everything I believed to be true is not. It is all false. My birth mother may still be alive – and it looks like she had three children, not five! What I believed to be true about the medical records has turned out to be false. So, I don't know anything about my birth mother's medical history.*

Also, the Adoption Authority released my birth certificate under false pretences. In fact, if my birth mother is still alive, she might be legally able to object to it having been released. OMG, what a mess! I feel so let down – by the whole system.

I mentioned my feelings to Mary earlier and she agreed with me. She finally agreed they had "found" the wrong woman. She was extremely apologetic for putting me through all the highs and lows I have endured over the last twelve months. And she admitted to also being very frustrated – because, of course, she now has to start her search from scratch for the second time.

I had been searching for two years and had hit two complete dead ends. I felt emotionally drained. One minute I had not only two potential brothers but four. The next, they had to start all over again, from scratch, because they had been looking at the wrong date of birth for my birth mother. And then, after that, they had been wasting months tracing the wrong woman altogether. So, I don't have four siblings and the woman they had found was not my birth mother. But on a positive note: My birth mother could still be alive.

I had endured the grieving process and had come to terms with the fact that I would never get to meet my birth mother, only to be told that they had found the wrong person and that this meeting could, possibly, still happen! Common sense should have prevailed, months ago! Instead I was encouraged to believe that everything that TUSLA had "found" was true, even though I made my own doubts quite clear. I felt so upset and disappointed – I felt so let down.

In the meantime, while still trying to digest everything, I decided to get in touch with the social worker overseeing my file at the Contact Preference Register. I asked him to check, even to double-check, the files regarding myself and my siblings. I asked him to check the signatures on the affidavits and to give me as much information as he was allowed to.

I still wasn't giving up.

Chapter 23

It was the morning of April 26th, 2016, when the social worker from the Contact Register phoned me. We discussed recent events and developments and the mix-up in my case. As I felt I wasn't getting anywhere with Mary, my social worker, I asked Ben to double-check the signatures on the signed affidavits for my siblings and me.

He confirmed that it was recorded that three babies had been born in and around Sean Ross Abbey. Baby one – me – had been born on April 20th 1969, as we know. Baby two had been born in 1974, a healthy baby and a normal delivery. Baby three had been born in 1975, in the vicinity of Sean Ross Abbey, and had been put up for a private adoption. (To be fair, Mary had mentioned this when I had met her in February.) A private adoption generally meant an adoption by a close friend or relative. It was also the youngest, "baby three", who had signed up to the Contact Register, registering a wish to get in touch with his siblings or birth parents.

Ben also confirmed that the signatures on the affidavits are the same. Even though the names on my admissions form and consent form are different, the signatures still look the same. (As already noted, my birth mother had chosen to put a shortened version of her name on the consent form.) He also confirmed that my adoption order had been issued in April 1970.

I told Ben about Mary "finding" the wrong birth mother and asked him to ensure that I'd been issued with the correct birth certificate; I had been worrying about this ever since discovering I'd been given false information. I had also been sleeping badly, as I kept imagining that the Adoption Authority had issued me with the wrong birth certificate. I kept thinking *Had I really found out my true identity in the Central Register Office that day in 2014?*

Ben soberly told me that "nothing was certain, as Mary needed to start her search again, wipe the slate clean and start afresh". So, yet again, I was living in terrible doubt. No one, it seemed, could confirm that the birth certificate I had been given was correct. What a nightmare! We were truly back to square one, and for the third time.

I also asked Ben if he would continue to try to locate my younger sibling, the so-called "baby three". (He had been trying to locate him, of course, because it had been believed that my birth mother had died.) Now that this was no longer certain I was told that the search for my potential brother must be put on hold until the correct woman was identified. I was very annoyed about this, as I made clear:

Apr 27 at 5:00 PM

Hi Ben,

A quick question for you. I received my birth certificate only after it was felt that my correct birth mother had been identified. Can we be sure that the birth certificate definitely relates to me?

Alice

Apr 29 at 8:17 AM

Hi Alice,

Apologies for the delay in replying. I was out of the office yesterday.
Until Mary establishes the exact identity of your birth mother we can't be sure.
I understand this is very difficult for you, but Mary is very thorough and will put every effort into identifying who she is.

Regards

Ben

Apr 29 at 2:12 PM

Hi Ben,

Thanks for that. Does this mean that you have stopped the search at your end? Presumably with the question marks hanging over my information we can no longer be certain that the two individuals that you have identified are my siblings?

Alice

Date: 3 May 2016 at 08:35:59 BST
To:
Subject: Re: Birth Certificate

Hi Alice,

Until Mary can verify the actual identity of your birth mother I am on hold.

Regards
Ben

May 3 at 12:33 PM

Ben,

Checking back through my notes, my birth name has been confirmed on a number of occasions, so I do not understand why you must now stop searching for my 2 siblings. The issue as I see it is that there is doubt over my birth mother's details, not my own. This is being dealt with by Mary. From what you have told me the signatures on all 3 affidavits are the same, therefore logic dictates that we are indeed siblings (irrespective of the name of our common birth mother).

My understanding is that your department is completely separate from Mary's. So, I don't understand why you are now having to wait on the outcome of her investigations when previously your investigation was separate. I would therefore ask again for you to continue your search.

Alice

On Tuesday, 3 May 2016,

Hi Alice,

Until Mary is able to verify the actual identity of your birth mother I am on hold.

Regards

Ben

And this turned out to be the case. I spoke to Mary in her office and she said that, even though the Contact Register in the Adoption Authority is separate from her department, we still needed to wait until the correct birth mother is found, as we required her permission before her offspring could attempt to get in touch with one another.

Below is an email sent to me from the department, explaining the procedures that they had to go through:

May 30 at 3:30 PM

Hi Alice,

I am glad you got home safely after our meeting last Saturday 28th May. As discussed in our chat today the following is an extract from The Adoption Board, Standardised Framework for the Provision of a National Information and Tracing Service, S15 Siblings/Relatives:

Siblings and Other Relatives

While there is no current legislative requirement to provide and information and tracing service to adult siblings, natural siblings, (adopted or non-adopted) or others, the Adoption Board considers that adult siblings, if they enquire should have a right to know of each other's existence.

Efforts must be made to inform the natural mother of any requests for contact between the adopted person and other members of the birth family.

- *All enquirers must be informed that only non-identifying information can be released without efforts being made to locate the natural mother and inform her of the enquiry.*
- *The natural mother does not have the right of veto on the release of information of the pursuance of a tracing enquiry.*
- *In the event that a natural mother feels strongly that a tracing service should not be provided she may apply to the Adoption Board via the placing agency outlining her reasons. The Adoption Board will then consider the matter and decide on the application.*

(Note - The above refers to the Adoption Board. The Adoption Board is now known as The Adoption Authority of Ireland since the implementation of the 2010 Adoption Act.)

Kind regards

Mary

I was truly angry upon receiving this. I thought *Why do we need our birth mother's permission? She gave all three of us away. She didn't want us! Yet, we still have to ask her permission, out of respect. And because it's the protocol.* The mind boggled. It seemed to me that the authorities almost enjoyed continually putting new hurdles in my way. Here was my own brother wanting to meet me – and me longing to meet him – both of us mature adults – and we could still be kept apart?

I also received an email from Mary, saying that she had started her search again. She told me that she was in the process of looking for a woman she had originally tried to find back in 2014 but had then discounted, for some reason that she was unable to share with me.

This refusal, as far as I was concerned, simply put the icing on the cake. I kept thinking *if only she had done her job properly in the first place, I wouldn't have had to endure the last two years of stress. . . and she was still withholding information from me?*

Chapter 24

As I wrote in May 2016: *So, here we go again. Back to square one for the third time. We can only hope that we do not hit another impasse.*

I feel totally drained and very disheartened. I have lost my faith in the system. Not that I had much in the first place. I feel that the department and its social workers make everything deliberately difficult, for themselves and for me. It feels almost as if they don't want me to succeed. Well, I am not giving up. I may be down, but I am by no means out. If I can't find my birth mother, I am determined to find my younger brother – as he at least is looking for me!

I'd had another thought too. I had been thinking about the baptismal records for Sean Ross Abbey being kept in Killaloe in Ennis. But where were the patient records kept? Tusla in Drogheda keep the records for Stamullen and the North East general area. I did some digging and found out that the files for Sean Ross Abbey were kept in the Tusla office in Waterford. I practically kicked myself. I'd been concentrating so hard on the records from Stamullen that I hadn't even considered Sean Ross Abbey. They might only have the same information as Tusla in Drogheda, but it was worth a try.

I wrote to Tusla in Waterford. A week or so afterwards, I received a letter in the post confirming that the information was as I had suspected. (Never mind. I had to cover all avenues.)

Later I wrote: *Feeling very exasperated. Mary is not replying to my emails. I phoned her team leader today, May 6th, 2016, expressing how upset and disappointed I was at being ignored yet again. I also told her how angry I was about the way my case had been handled. That the social worker has come to not just one dead end but two. That she sent me on an emotional rollercoaster ride to no purpose. That she gave me medical information that turned out to be false. And - most of all - that I'd had to emotionally deal with finding my true identity – only to be told that the information I'd been given was all incorrect.*

The team leader to whom I had complained in October 2015 had been moved on, for reasons unexplained. There was now a new team leader. I hoped that she had more energy than her predecessor!

I asked her if she could make my case a priority. She said "that she would, and would go a step further and get three members of the team on to it". I hoped she would be true to her word!

9th of May 2016.

I had a phone call from Mary today. I had been expecting it after my phone call to her team leader. She asked how I was feeling, as she was aware, I had spoken to her supervisor. I told her exactly how I was feeling. How upset and frustrated I was at the lack of compassion shown by TUSLA. (Luckily for me, I am thick-skinned. If I'd been soft, I'm not sure I could have taken these knock-backs. Especially after having been led to believe my birth mother was deceased and I had four siblings. Now, of course, none of that is true.) She reassured me my case had been made a priority. I asked to be updated as and when the new information came in. I also asked if she could send me a report on what has been done in the search so far. (I mainly requested this because Mary often gets confused.) I said that I would much prefer to have everything put in writing, so that I could refer back to it. She was very hesitant about this, and even tried to put me off by saying it would be the end of June before she could manage to do it. . . This report never arrived. Luckily, I kept my diaries!

Mary also told me that she had managed to locate the social worker who had dealt with the private adoption of my youngest sibling. This woman cannot recall my birth mother, or even organising the private adoption. However, she was quite elderly, so we couldn't expect her to remember all the mothers and babies with whom she had come into contact.

Mary also asked when I was next travelling to Ireland, as she and the new team leader would like to meet up with me. I told her that I was booked to travel to Ireland at the end of the month and eagerly asked if she had any new information for me. *(Could this be the reason she wanted to meet up?)* She insisted that there weren't any updates; it was simply that her team leader would like to meet with me, face-to-face. I found this a bit bizarre. I had planned on going home to Ireland to spend the weekend with my mum and sister, to celebrate my sister's fiftieth birthday. I didn't really want to have to traipse over to Drogheda just, so Mary's new team leader could suss me out!

Yet Mary – or rather her team leader? – seemed determined to meet me, even though they didn't have any new information. This did not feel right. When I told them my flight times they even asked if we could meet in Dublin airport on that Friday night. *Really!? When they didn't have any new information for me?*

I wasn't buying any of this. I spoke to my sister and updated her on the latest developments. She was also very suspicious.

On May 23rd, 2016, the week before I was due to fly to Ireland, I emailed Mary to see if anything new had emerged. She insisted that the team leader wanted to meet me just, wait for it, to see my face. I couldn't believe it. My sister believed that they were hiding new information, something which they didn't want to tell me over the phone. Instead they were leaving me guessing and sending my mind into overdrive, thinking all sorts. When I reminded Mary of the dates and times of my flights, she asked if I could meet with her and her team leader in the Drogheda office on Saturday morning, May 28th.

Still no new developments, allegedly! But I still questioned why they would want to meet on a Saturday, when the government offices are closed. They were opening the offices specially to meet me, and they didn't have any new information? – This all felt very strange. Were they really trying to fool me into believing they had nothing new to tell me?! Honestly, after dealing with them for over two years, I think I knew them a bit better than that!

I think I need to recap the events since February 2016.

Mary was looking at two women with the same name. She eliminated one woman, as she was ten years older than the details on the non-identifying information. We then found out that this woman was deceased.

Mary then decided to search for a woman who had given two names. Mary seemed to think this woman had given false names as she signed the admissions form with a long name and the consent form with a shortened version of the same name. (I firmly believed that this was the same person. She just used the shortened version as she probably used it more often.) As far as Mary was aware this woman was also deceased. (And yet, if this were the case, why hadn't she asked for a death certificate and cause of death the first time she'd checked her out?) Mary had stopped looking for this woman initially because she didn't fit some criteria she had. (I was unsure what information didn't tally, for example date of birth, address etc., as I wasn't privy to that information.)

Mary then focused on the woman living in the UK who also shared the same name. (There were three women with the same name, in all.) The name she was looking for was Margaret or Maggie, for short. It is of course a quite common name and I was also warned by Mary that it is not unknown for some members of the same family to share the same first name.

Now Mary has gone back to focusing on the woman who had signed with two versions of the same name: Margaret and Maggie. (I wondered if she had messed up the first-time round, somehow, and had only just realised it?) I had asked her repeatedly why she had given up looking for this woman in the first place. What had come to light since that has caused her to reconsider? I was given no response to my questions. I was completely ignored.

On Friday evening, the 28th of May 2016, I travelled home to Ireland to spend the weekend with my mum. We should have been celebrating my sister and my first cousin's 50th birthday, but the party had unluckily been cancelled, due to my sister's mother-in-law having passed away. (I had decided to fly home anyway. No point in wasting a plane ticket! Also, it wasn't just me flying over. One cousin had arrived from southern England that same morning.)

My sister and mum met me at the airport. Our only topic of conversation was why Mary wanted to meet so urgently. We kept going over all the possibilities on the journey to my mum's house. As I wrote the next morning:

I didn't get a lot of sleep last night. All I could think about was the sudden urgency to meet, especially when they didn't have anything new for me. My gut instinct is telling me that they are keeping something from me. I have been doing this search for too long now not to know when Mary and her colleagues are hiding something from me.

I also awoke early and could not get back to sleep! – I had a million and one things going through my mind. I had breakfast with my mum, just a cup of tea. I could not eat as my stomach was churning. I just do not know what to think. Has Mary made a breakthrough, but will not tell me until she meets me face-to-face? Are they still trying to suss me out? Are they trying to decide if I am of sound mind? Is it going to be a counselling session? I won't be happy if it is. I didn't travel to Ireland to have my weekend interrupted for a counselling session. Not only did I fly from England for this, but it also takes over an hour from my mum's house to get to the office in Drogheda.

The meeting was at noon. My sister picked my mum and me up early. The conversation in the car naturally centred round the meeting and around various possible scenarios as to why they wanted to meet me. I felt excited, but I was trying not to get my hopes up because previous experience had taught me that whatever hopes I had could be shattered without a second thought.

We arrived with time to spare that hot summer's afternoon. My sister and I were both attending the meeting, as I had asked for my sister to be present, as an extra pair of ears. The last couple of meetings I had been on my own and I had found that Mary later backtracked on what she had said previously or else couldn't remember it. This was why I have kept meticulous diaries and saved all our correspondence.

I phoned Mary to let her know we had arrived. She came out to meet us and guided us to a very dated, dark little room. I couldn't help thinking: *The whole building needs updating or knocking down.*

Mary and her team leader, who were conducting the meeting, sat on normal hard chairs while my sister and I sat on exceptionally low soft chairs. I felt as if we were young children in the school principal's office, being told off!

Once we'd got the pleasantries out of the way, they proceeded to tell me they were looking at three women aged nineteen, twenty and twenty-two at the time of my birth. They had also found a new woman with the same name. (So, they had "no new information" for me. Really!)

They had sent a letter to this newly-discovered woman on Monday the 23rd of May, the Monday before I had arrived back in Ireland – and the day I'd spoken to Mary on the phone. Why on earth couldn't she have told me this when I'd asked if she had any updates for me? – This was so infuriating. They could have saved me a lot of stress and sleepless nights. I was not impressed with the way the authorities were handling my case. If I asked about any new developments, I expected to be told the truth. I did not expect to be lied to.

Anyway, they had sent this woman a letter, and she had phoned Mary on Tuesday and left a voicemail message. Mary had phoned her back and asked her some open questions. This woman had appeared very confident that she had only ever had two babies, both born after her marriage. So, Mary had decided to disregard this woman. (Fine, but why all the secrecy? She could have told me this on the phone a week ago!)

The team leader mentioned that this woman and the woman on my non-identifying information lived in the same area, as well as sharing the same name. The team leader let slip the name of the area and was very embarrassed when she realised her mistake. (This was a major error, for which she could possibly be disciplined or even sacked.) She immediately begged me not to go knocking on doors there looking for my birth mother as we were unaware of her current circumstances: for example, her husband or family might not know about me or even about what her life had been like, 47 years ago.

After her mistake, my sister and I took advantage, and started firing questions at the team leader. She admitted that the area they were looking at was 11 km from Sean Ross Abbey. (I will not identify the area here, out of respect for my birth mother's privacy, however, this slip of the tongue fitted the information I had.) My birth mother had gone into labour eight weeks early and had been admitted to Sean Ross Abbey that same day. The team leader also mentioned that my birth mother had previously been given a blood test in a Limerick hospital but that her blood group was not on the test result.

I was unsure that I believed this, even though my youngest sibling had been privately adopted from Limerick Hospital. All this information was in that thick blue file: the file I was not privy to. Yet still when I tripped them up the information just seemed to emerge!

Mary then asked me, again, to consider searching for the siblings of the woman who had lived in the UK but who was now deceased. I was unsure why she asked me to do this. I thought we had drawn a line under that potential candidate and moved on. (Well I had moved on, at any rate. I refused to believe that she wasn't the right woman, as she'd had another baby only five-and-a-half month after I was born.)

We had officially ruled her out, back in April. Mary sometimes needed to think about what she was saying, and to check her notes before speaking. I sometimes got the impression that she just wanted me to passively agree with everything she said, so that she could simply close my file. I told myself *No chance. I am in this for the long haul.*

Mary had asked the priest, from 2014, to investigate all three of these women (they had all lived in the same locality, so this should have been easy). The secretary of the school in the area was also going to check old school records, to see if she could find anything. I suspected that Mary had yet another person in mind, but that she wasn't letting on. The truth was, I was only ever told anything on a strictly need-to-know basis!

We spoke about Father Reagan and Stamullen. We discussed the meeting I had had with him when I was nineteen, the meeting that had lasted all of five minutes. I mentioned how abrupt and dismissive he was. How he told me to be grateful for what I have. What a very unpleasant man he had been!

We also spoke about the fond memories my sister and I retained of the Stamullen Mother and Baby Home, and how we'd used to visit the nuns and babies as we were growing up. (Mary appeared visibly shocked by this. I was unsure why, as I had mentioned our visits to Stamullen in previous meetings.) How my 5th-year class had donated money to the Mother and Baby Home and how well-liked Sister Marie Louise had been. How I didn't have any bad memories of Stamullen.

The social workers said they were widening their search of the area that the team leader let slip. The team leader remained utterly mortified that she had let out this delicate piece of information. She kept asking me – over and over – to be sensitive towards my birth mother, to respect her privacy and not to attempt to visit her home place. She urged me to let the Mary locate her and to break the news to her about my searching for her, and – potentially – finding her. I think she was extremely concerned about how her error could rebound on her, and how even her job might perhaps be at stake. I assured her (again) that I had no intention of tracking my potential birth mother down or of knocking on her door unexpectedly.

At the end of the meeting Mary asked me if she could take a photograph of me on her phone. I found this a rather odd request but agreed. She said she simply wanted to have an up-to-date photograph on file. I hadn't known that they had a photograph of me in the first place! I couldn't help thinking *Is there something else she's not telling me?*

We had a two-hour meeting – it was very intense. My sister and I were completely drained when we came out. I was so grateful that my sister had been with me as an extra pair of ears because she had witnessed, first-hand, how the social worker contradicted what she was saying. She could finally understand what I had been dealing with over the past two years. As for me, I vowed not to doubt myself anymore.

After the meeting, my mum, my sister and I headed to a nice restaurant for a late lunch. We had a lovely meal as we analysed the two-hour meeting. My mum was completely intrigued, but then, she had been involved in this search from day one. Her support meant a great deal to me. I don't think I could have done all that I managed to do, had she objected. I knew I hadn't offended her in any way: I knew she understood my reasons. She has just been wonderful.

We arrived back at my mum's house late that afternoon, and in the evening my sister and I headed out to the local pub, to reconnect with various friends and cousins. We had a great night catching up with everyone.

I spent the next day with my mum and my sister's family. We enjoyed a traditional roast beef dinner before I flew back to the UK on the evening of Sunday, the 29th of May.

As I wrote in my diary: *I'm not sure how I feel. There is certainly a possibility that one of these women is my birth mother. To be honest, I am trying hard not to conjure up stories in my head. I've had so many highs and lows that I don't know how much more I can take. Do you remember my mentioning that you need to be thick-skinned and have plenty of family and friends around you to go through this process? Now, you can probably understand why!*

Chapter 25

June 1st, 2016

I travelled back to Manchester last night on a Ryanair flight. What a full but tiring weekend! It was great seeing everyone. Especially those cousins I have not seen in years.

I'm up early because Alex has a GCSE exam today and I haven't seen him all weekend, though I have been in contact with him via FaceTime and text. I feel a bit bad about that, but it couldn't be helped. He fully understands. He has gone to school to sit his exam and I'm trying to catch up on some work I missed on Friday.

As my morning went on, trying to juggle housework with working for our business, I received a phone call from Mary. I'd last spoke to her only 48 hours previously. Surely, she couldn't have new information for me already? Well, she had. She proceeded to tell me that she had located yet another woman who fits the criteria on file for my birth mother.

A letter has been sent out to this woman today – hopefully, she will respond.

I am trying not to get my hopes up as I have been let down too many times in the past. I'm not sure I can take much more of this emotional rollercoaster ride. I would like to get off it soon – if I can.

That evening at 6:30, I was finishing dinner with Max and Alex, relaxing with a glass of wine, when I received a text from Mary. The timing was unusual, as she finished work at 5.30. Why was she texting me this late? The text asked me to phone her back straightaway, on her home number. I turned to Max and said, "This is weird. Mary wants me to phone her on her home number."

Imagine what was going through my head. I started to actually shake with excitement – though I also felt wary, as I had been let down so often in the past. I'm not sure how I held the phone steady enough to dial her number on my way out of the room.

I went into our office, as I did not want Alex to see me upset. I certainly didn't want him distracted, in the middle of his GCSE exams. Mary answered the phone immediately, sounding very upbeat. She told me triumphantly that she had found my birth mother. I was standing up at the time and very nearly collapsed. I couldn't believe what I was hearing. *Was this for real? Did she really have the right person, after all this time?*

Later, I wrote: *My birth mother received Mary's letter today and phoned Mary at 4.30 p.m. They were on the phone until 5.10 p.m. Her name, as we knew, is Margaret.*

Mary asked no leading questions, but Margaret confirmed that she had given birth to a little girl on the 20th of April 1969 in Sean Ross Abbey and that her name was Catherine Ann.

Now Catherine Ann had been the name my birth mother had given me. It was my parents who had called me Alice.

The moment I heard these words I completely broke down. Max could see me through the window and ran straight to me. I was so consumed by emotion I could not even speak. Two years after the search had begun, I had finally found my birth mother and she was alive – not dead, as I was led to believe. What a turnaround! Meanwhile, Mary was still on the phone. She kept talking about her conversation with Margaret.

She told me that Margaret was incredibly happy that I had found her. She had said that she had always thought about me, especially on my birthday and at Christmastime. She had always wondered if I got nice presents. She had always hoped I'd been adopted by nice people and had grown up in a loving family environment. She had never forgotten me and would even have searched for me, except that she had believed that she couldn't. She had been led to believe by the nuns, when she gave me away, that she would not be allowed to look for me later in life.

Upon hearing this I burst into tears: two years of built-in stress and emotion was finally released. Indeed, it wasn't just two years – it was 47 years. Forty-seven years of wondering. Wondering why she gave me away. Wondering if she was still alive. Wondering where she was. Wondering if she ever thought about me. I couldn't hold it in any longer. I sat with my husband and son and tried, again and again, to calm down, but I could not stop crying. Every time I tried to talk; I broke down.

Mary also gave me a little information about Margaret, from their forty-minute phone conversation.

Margaret had given birth to me when she was only twenty. (That bit I already knew.) She had herself been adopted and had loved her adoptive parents very much. She had been an only child, and, while pregnant with me, her adoptive father was dying of cancer. (He died in October,1969.) She had never told him that she was pregnant – but she still believed that he knew. Her father had been in hospital when she had been admitted to Sean Ross Abbey. Her mother had wanted her to bring me home, but she had refused, because they would not have been able to provide for me properly: they wouldn't have been able to give me a good life. I am profoundly grateful to Margaret for making that difficult decision because, of course, I did have an incredibly good upbringing – nobody could have asked for better. I have been blessed to have been adopted, not only into my immediate family, but also into my extended family.

Margaret's own mother had died seventeen years after I was born, aged 94. They had always been very close. Margaret still lives in the house where she grew up.

Margaret also spoke to Mary, at least a little, about Sean Ross Abbey. She told Mary that my birth father had paid for her to be admitted as a private patient. He had paid £100 to the nuns. She didn't experience any abuse from the nuns because she'd been a private patient – but she'd observed the cruelties other women had suffered. When she entered Sean Ross Abbey she was given a "house name": Agatha. She was also known as "a first offender". (The women there were never referred to by their proper names.) She remembered Sister Hildegarde and Sister Frances: Sister Frances worked in the laundry while Sister Hildegarde had signed her affidavit. These were the two nuns depicted in Philomena. It still makes me shiver every time I think about it.

Margaret also remembered taking me to Dublin, in my birth father's car, and handing me over to two nuns underneath Clerys Clock. She even remembered dressing me in a little lemon-coloured outfit that she had been obliged to buy from the Sean Ross Abbey shop.

I still own a photograph of me with my dad and my sister on the day mum and dad picked me up from Stamullen and – yes – I was wearing a lemon-coloured outfit.

Apparently, the unmarried mothers used to work during the week for pennies; and then, when the time came for their babies to be taken away, they were made to buy the clothes from the shop in Sean Ross Abbey so that their money went back to the nuns. Basically, the nuns profited, no matter what.

Two years after Margaret's mother died, she married her husband. They have been happily married since 1988 and have one son, my half-brother. They also have one granddaughter, with another grandchild due at the end of July.

I asked Mary if Margaret had mentioned my two brothers whom she'd also given up for adoption. She hadn't. Mary seemed to believe that Margaret was in denial about them both.

Margaret did apparently say that she wanted to meet me and that she had never stopped thinking about me – but, first, she needed to tell her husband and son that I'd found her. You see, she had told her husband when she met him that she'd had a daughter and had given her up for adoption.

The reason she'd told him all those years ago was because she heard the song "Nobody's Child" on the radio and had immediately broken down in tears. This song apparently brought back painful memories because the nuns had asked for this song to be sung in Sean Ross Abbey when the women put on concerts as entertainment. (There seemed no end to their cruelty!) When Mary told me this I started crying myself, because I remembered my own sister singing this song at family functions.

As a young child I'd used to cry myself to sleep with this song going around and round my head, wondering where my birth mother was and why she had given me away. I still remember the words and they still make me sad, thinking about the effect they'd had on my childhood – and, once I learned about it, from Mary, also on my birth mother herself.

Margaret's husband said that he would have helped her to find me but that they honestly believed that they couldn't. She's never told her son about me. She needed to tell her son about my finding her before she could agree to meet me: she didn't want to keep secrets from either of them. Yet she had also told Mary that she had secretly hoped that I would one day come looking for her. I felt emotionally overwhelmed by this, especially after years of wondering if she would ever want to meet me or if she would prefer to keep me as some dirty little secret.

The topic of my birth father did arise. I was interested to know about his family background, but Margaret was apparently hesitant to talk about him and very reluctant to give out any information. According to Mary, she seemed almost to clam up when his name was mentioned. When I heard this I thought: *Were the memories of him and their time together so horrific? Had he mistreated or abused her?*

The only bits of information given about my birth father was that he had been fifteen years my birth mother's senior, so he had been 35 when I was born. Also, Margaret told Mary that he had died, aged 65, of a brain haemorrhage. That was all she was willing to share. As time passed, I hoped she might open up a bit more.

Mary believed that Margaret was traumatised by her whole experience. After all, she had hidden her secrets for almost half a century. So, for me to come looking for her has probably come as quite a shock. I also had to remember that much of what she had blanked out of her mind must have resurfaced in a rush. I really felt sorry for my birth mother: perhaps the last thing she needed, at her age, was to feel frightened that her past might come back to haunt her. I also completely understood that she needed to tell her family.

Margaret asked Mary what my name was now, and Mary gave her the longer version of my first name. I didn't really feel comfortable about giving out much information about myself at this stage. I suspected that I would feel better about it after I met her. If only that ever happened!

Mary suggested that I write a letter to Margaret, which I agreed to do. I hoped it would ease her mind a little and make her a bit more relaxed.

As the telephone conversation between Mary and me drew to a close she reminded me that my birth mother would need time to digest the latest events. She was thrilled that I'd found her and wanted to meet me, but she needed time to tell her husband and son. (She had told her husband, years ago, that she had given up a daughter for adoption, but this had never been mentioned since. She had never told him about the two sons she had given up for adoption.) She also had a grandchild due and was already committed to helping her son and daughter-in-law at this manic, exciting time. Mary even hinted that Margaret might need counselling and support to get her through this. She was clearly very anxious and worried about her husband and son finding out her secrets. (Of course, I wasn't the only secret she had. She had two more secrets hidden away.) Apparently, she lived in fear that her husband and son might desert her, leaving her all alone in her final years. I totally understood her anxiety and promised to give her as much time and space as she needed. (After all, I'd waited over four decades. A few more weeks or months couldn't make much difference!)

I thought: *I think Margaret sounds overwhelmed by the fact that I have tracked her down. I think she is in a state of shock and may even be traumatised. I don't think she can believe I want to meet her. She has kept me a secret for so long and kept all emotions regarding me bottled up inside, so I'm not sure how she is going to deal with the secret coming out, especially to her son. Will she ever tell her husband and son that I found her? That has to be the question.*

She must have conflicting emotions. She must feel happy and excited, that a weight had been lifted, that her long-lost daughter had found her. The daughter she always thought about on her birthday and at Christmastime. But she might still be feeling ashamed of having given birth to an illegitimate child in a Catholic society. She is probably terrified of what people might think – not only about me, but also about the other two secrets she has locked away. The two secrets her husband knows nothing about. She must worry that she may lose the good name and respect she's built up for herself since she married her husband and put my birth father behind her.

I turned to my husband and son and started to cry, yet again. I was in such shock. I really couldn't get my head around what had just happened. I couldn't believe I had finally done it. I had found her. I had achieved what I'd begun to think was the impossible. Max was great – but then, both he and Alex had been so supportive throughout this whole process! They had always been there for me.

Once I finally managed to pull myself together, I phoned my sister and told her my news, though I don't think she could really understand what I was saying between the sobs. She was very happy for me because she'd been starting to worry about the effect all the disappointments had been having on me. This breakthrough meant that I had already learned things about my history and the first three weeks of my life that I'd never known before. It was only basic information, but it was a start.

I eventually went to bed, but of course I couldn't sleep. My mind was racing with questions. I was feeling overwhelmed by everything. I kept thinking I found her. I found her! And I was so weepy: I just couldn't stop crying. Decades of tears escaped from my eyes. There was no holding them back.

The next day I phoned Mum and told her what happened. She was thrilled for me. I also asked her if she could remember what I was wearing the day she and Daddy had picked me up from Stamullen. She couldn't – however, I hadn't thought it likely that she would as it was so long ago, and she was, after all, 85. I asked if she had any photographs of me from that day – and she had. My sister rooted one out and texted it to me and – yes – I was wearing a lemon-coloured outfit. My dad was holding me in one arm – I looked so tiny! – and my sister was sitting on his other knee, with his other arm around her. It was hard to believe that this man in the photograph was not my birth father.

But he will always be my dad. That can never change.

Chapter 26

I had spoken to my sister on the evening of the 6th of June, and we discussed the meeting we'd had with the social workers in May and how Mary had taken two photographs of me with her mobile phone. Then, only a few days later I'd been told that she had found a woman fitting the criteria we'd been looking for. I hoped she hadn't shown my birth mother my photograph without my permission. I still suspected that Mary had known about Margaret when she asked to meet me in Drogheda on May 28th – and that she decided not to tell me about her at that point, for some reason.

If my guess was correct, why the delay? Why hadn't I been told about her when we were arranging to meet? I'd found that this had happened a lot in the last two years, and I'd learned that TUSLA always had to be seen to be in control. It really wasn't fair, because I don't think that some people in my position could have coped with their deliberate withholding of information, which was not only infuriating but also played havoc with one's mind. I felt – I still feel – that the Irish government needs to change the way they dealt with people and should cultivate more understanding about the mixed emotions that adoptees go through.

I finally wrote a letter to Margaret, giving some basic information about myself.

Margaret,

I wanted to give you a little bit of background information on me.

I grew up as part of a family of five. Both my older sister and younger brother were also adopted. I had an incredibly happy upbringing and feel privileged to be a part of my immediate and extended family. My mum is one of fifteen and my dad was one of six. So, cousins were always in abundance!

I have been happily married for sixteen-and-a-half years and have one son, who is fifteen. My husband and I run our own business and live in North West England.

You were always in my thoughts as I was growing up, but I finally decided to search for you in May 2014. It has been a long two years but with Mary's help, and with help from her colleagues, we eventually found you. I am travelling home to Ireland in July for one week and would like (and hope) to meet up with you.

I sent the letter off to Mary by recorded delivery on the 13th of June as she needed to read it before Margaret could see it. I was hoping that Margaret could receive it before I went away on holiday (on the 24th). I also mentioned to Mary that I would be in Ireland for a week in July and that I would be happy to meet Margaret then.

However, Mary was away until the 20th of June, so I simply had to wait and see.
On the 20th of June, I waited anxiously to hear from Mary, as I longed to know if she had received the letter destined for Margaret.

As I was catching up on some accounting work, I received an email from Mary to say that she had returned from her holiday and that my letter had arrived. I emailed her to ask her to try and contact Margaret before the 24th, as Max, Alex and I were heading off to Mexico for a well-earned break, as Alex just finished his final GCSE exam.

I also asked her if she could possibly find out my birth father's name for me. My mind had been all over the place with various questions about him and his family. I was also keen to learn his name and where he was buried so that I could visit his grave.

I got no response to my email. It was only at the end of the working day that Mary phoned to tell me that she had spoken to Margaret. I'd been left wondering all day whether she was going to contact her: she could have at least emailed me to say she would try and reach her at some point during the day! This is yet another example of the social workers not taking the time to think about what I might be feeling at such a tense time. It is the "not knowing" that is so hard to deal with, and – after all – it only takes a minute to type out an email!

At any rate, Mary had visited Margaret in her home. She relayed the conversation to me in the phone call, and I recorded it in my notes:

Today Margaret told Mary that she does want to meet me but that she still hasn't told her husband that I've found her. Also, she hasn't told her son anything about me at all. He doesn't even know I exist. I don't believe she will ever tell him because she's so ashamed and embarrassed about her past and so terrified of losing him. I do understand her predicament and I do not hold it against her. But it is a shame to think that I may never meet my half-brother!

She also says she doesn't want to keep any secrets from her husband, and that she needs time to absorb recent events. After all, it has been very traumatic for her as well. She has had a lot to deal with in a short space of time. At least I'd had two years to prepare for this moment! In addition, the birth of her second grandchild is imminent and she is helping her daughter-in-law with her two-year-old, too. She needs time and has asked me to give her time. She doesn't think she can meet me in July. There is just too much going on in her life right now. It's such a shame because it would have been nice to meet when Max was with me and when we didn't have to worry about work. Never mind! – It cannot be helped. I asked Mary to ask Margaret to write me a letter. That way all of this could feel a bit more real for me.

My birth father was mentioned (in her conversation with Mary). She repeated that he had died of a brain haemorrhage at 65. His family knew about me – but didn't want anything to do with me. That was all she was willing to say. I suspect that my birth father's family were wealthy and of good standing in the community. They were probably worried about what their local society would think of an illegitimate child. Back then it was better to turn your back and wash your hands of the situation. I would like to know something about his family – what type of people they were and so on, but I am not sure if Margaret will ever open up about them.

On June 21st, I received an email from Mary, further explaining the difficult time Margaret was having in coming to terms with everything that had happened. She reminded me that I needed to be patient and to give Margaret time to digest all of this. It wasn't every day that the baby you gave away decades ago showed up and wanted to meet you, especially when you'd hidden your secret so successfully for so long! I thought *It isn't just me that she has to come to terms with, but two sons she'd given away. Surely, she must be thinking about them, too?*

Jun 21 at 10:07 AM

Hi Alice,

Thank you for your e-mail. I understand fully where your question is coming from in relation to your sense of identity. When I meet with your birth mother, I will put that question to her and when she is in a position to give me his name I will let you know. All of this is very new for her at this stage of her life and she will need time to unlock the memories and secrets she has kept over the forty-seven years in a safe and predictable environment which is right for her. She will need time also to bring her family into this huge life event which she is really happy has begun for both of you in a positive way for everyone involved.

She asked for time to think about all of this when I spoke with her yesterday and we agreed that unless I heard from her before 4th of July we will meet and chat about you both establishing contact in that week.

With best regards

Mary

I totally understood that Margaret needed time to come to terms with recent events. My only fear was that she would never find the courage to tell her husband and son about me.

If that turned out to be the case, I would have to deal with issues of rejection all over again.

Chapter 27

On July 5th Mary phoned, to say that she had met with Margaret in her home the previous day and had given Margaret the letter I had written for her. My birth mother was very appreciative, and incredibly pleased to hear that I have enjoyed a good and happy life.

Mary then had a counselling session with Margaret for two hours and she managed to learn a little more. For example, Margaret had admitted that, when she had gone into labour with me – eight weeks early, remember – she hadn't even realised that she was in labour – and neither had her mother! Mary seemed to think that the pregnancy had been concealed. I thought it likely that my birth mother had been in denial about her condition, and that her own mother – for whatever reason – hadn't noticed. It seemed to have been only my birth father who had realised what was really happening. He'd driven Margaret to Sean Ross Abbey, a short drive from where she lived – and where she still lives, as I knew because the team leader accidentally let Margaret's location slip in our meeting, back in May.

At the Abbey my birth father had paid £100 to the nuns, so that Margaret could be admitted as a private patient. Then, after dropping her off that Sunday night, he had headed back to the church hall in the village, to play snooker with the priest. (You just couldn't make it up!) Meanwhile Margaret – only twenty, naïve, scared, in labour, and probably not understanding what was happening to her body – had been left entirely on her own in that terrible place. While at the same time her own father – whom she loved dearly – was in hospital with cancer. What a nightmare for her!

My non-identifying information claimed that I had been breastfed, yet Margaret told Mary that she had not been allowed to hold me the whole of the three weeks in Sean Ross Abbey. Instead, she'd had to use a breast pump to express her milk and the nuns or nurses had bottle-feed me. How distressing for her! – yet she had coped somehow, and three weeks later she and my birth father had transported me to Dublin. He had driven Margaret to Dublin with two nuns from Sean Ross Abbey in the backseat as chaperones, while she had been in the passenger seat, holding me. That journey to Dublin was the longest period Margaret ever held me. And when they got to Dublin, she handed me over to two nuns from Stamullen, underneath Clerys Clock. *(What must she have been feeling?)*

Margaret had also apparently mentioned my birth father, giving us slightly more information than before. They had met when she was just fifteen: he was thirty. They had lived in the same village. He was an important figure in the local church and also a pioneer. ("Pioneers" abstain from drinking alcohol). Despite this, he never married and was actually living with another woman all the while he'd been with Margaret.

I had so many questions! I didn't know if Margaret had stayed with him until her mother died or if they'd gone their separate ways after my youngest brother was born (in 1975). Also: what kind of a man could my father have been, to have slept with Margaret when she was only fifteen, and – at the same time – be living with another unmarried woman? Had he been controlling her all the while? – and perhaps even treating the other woman in the same way? I hated what I was thinking that he might have been a manipulator, someone who'd had some sort of hold over my birth mother. Was it possible that she had been too scared to leave him? Questions, questions!

Margaret has given Mary – to give to me, at some point – a black-and-white photograph of my birth father with his arm around her, taken on Margaret's 21st birthday. Apparently, there is a birthday cake before them, with a silver "21" on it and they're both holding a knife, ready to cut the cake. Her twenty-first would have been in June,1969. So, it appeared that my birth father had thrown a twenty-first birthday party for my birth mother less than two months after I'd been born and given away for adoption. Surely, Margaret would still have been in mourning for the loss of her baby? I truly doubt that she would have been in a party mood! . . . What a strong person she must have been, so young and so uneducated, to have carried off the fiction that everything was normal in her life!

Margaret has given Mary this photo, but she didn't want me to see it – at least, not yet – because she feared that I would go to her home village and start making enquiries (in case neighbours, for example, might be able to recognise my birth parents from the photo). She was still terrified about her secrets coming out. So, Mary – though she could describe it to me – could not show me the photo until Margaret gave her permission.

This was utterly exasperating, as I really wanted to see it. To see who I looked like. I have been wondering for years whom I looked like! (I had also wondered, again and again, where my son gets his talent for music from.)

Mary also mentioned that there was a range cooker – a gift from my father – in Margaret's kitchen. So, from all that I could deduce, my birth father, a churchgoer, had money, a trade, a car, and a good standing in the local community. I suspected that Margaret had been attractive, shy and vulnerable and that he'd played on these attributes to take advantage of her. He'd bought her gifts, perhaps to make her feel wanted – or perhaps to make himself feel better, about getting her pregnant three times and perhaps pressurising her into giving up her babies.

As I wrote, *still almost disbelieving, that night: You see, Margaret also told Mary that my birth father was the father of my two younger brothers. So, they aren't my half-brothers. They are my full brothers. Oh, my word, I can't take all this in! I have two full brothers. Margaret has even given me permission to contact them! – She doesn't want any contact with them herself, though. I believe she's still in denial about having given birth to them. (Note: Mary also said that the baby boy born in 1974 was born in Sean Ross Abbey but the baby boy born in 1975 was not.)*

I later found out that neither baby boy could have been born in Sean Ross Abbey, as the Home closed in 1970. In fact, Mary has since learned that the elder was born in a hospital in Limerick, along with the baby born in 1975. The third baby had been adopted privately, as we already knew: Margaret seemed to recall that a friend of a neighbour adopted him. (I really didn't think that Mary should have been divulging this information to me, as it was not my information. It was my brother's information. However, I received it.)

It was my belief that Margaret was probably still in denial with regard to her two other babies because she'd never seen or held them. It was no surprise that she was still traumatised! She'd had three babies, had only ever held one of them and had given away all three. Probably the only reason she still remembered me was because she had held me, on that long, long journey to Dublin.

But why had she become pregnant again (and again) after having me? Well, we have to remember what Catholic Ireland was like in the late 1960s and early 70s. It was an intensely religious, very Catholic country, one basically ruled by the Church.

For example, Margaret had confided to Mary that, when she started her first period, her bedding had of course been ruined. She had rushed to tell her mum and all her mum had said was, "This will happen to you from now on, once a month." As I wrote later: *There was absolutely no explanation given to her about what was happening to her body. On hearing this I can understand why she fell pregnant on two more occasions. Back then, adoption was used as a form of birth control. What I still don't understand is why my birth father let it happen. What type of a man was he? I don't believe he was a good, honourable man. I just cannot believe that.*

Margaret had also told Mary that, when her first grandchild was born, and she had held her for the first time, she had instantly been reminded of me – the memories had just come flooding back from when she had held me, on that dreadful journey to Dublin. Apparently, she'd had a difficult time concealing her emotions from her family, while holding her first grandchild, that day.

Margaret had herself also been adopted, as we knew, but Mary has discovered that it had been an unlawful adoption. Apparently, she had simply been cast aside by her mother, and the district nurse had taken her away. The nurse had given her to her adoptive parents, but the adoption had never been legally registered. Which was why Mary could find no record of her. In fact, Mary was at present trying to find out the name Margaret's birth mother had chosen, so that she could get a birth certificate for her. How sad! – 68 years in the world and had never possessed a birth certificate! At least I had an adoption certificate!

But Margaret had never travelled outside Ireland, so she had never needed a passport. When she'd got married the parish priest had apparently sorted out a baptismal certificate for her, which had sufficed for the marriage.

As I wrote: *Mary is still relaying snippets of her conversation with Margaret. Judging by what she tells me, when Margaret was growing up she had a very hard life. She was always referred to as illegitimate, was called unpleasant names, and was treated contemptuously, like a second-class citizen. Such treatment at such a young age might very well have made anyone insecure and lacking in confidence. I suspect that, in her teens, she may have hungered to feel wanted and accepted, not treated like an outsider. Maybe my birth father gave her the security she so desperately craved – even though his real interests lay elsewhere.*

Mary said that Margaret walked every day and looked to be in good health. The only thing was, she smoked like a train! But she did not drink and neither did her husband. Margaret had asked Mary to find out if I could send her a baby photograph and also a more recent photograph of myself. I said that I would.

Mary also said that Margaret is willing to correspond with me without her son knowing who I am – but not without her husband's knowing. Wow, what a lot to take in! (Also: what a lot of information to come out of one meeting!)

All that evening I kept going over and over the conversation with Mary in my head. I also wrote it down in my diary, so I would be able to refer to it in the future. Of course, I also shared the updates in my story with Max. It was so good to be able to talk about it! – and Max can sometimes put a different perspective on things.

It was only when I went to bed that I started thinking again about my birth father and the type of man he was. I had so many questions that needed answering! – but I did not feel sure that I would ever get a chance to ask them.

The next morning (July 6th) I emailed Mary, asking if Margaret had mentioned my birth father's name or where he was buried. I was very keen to find out a little bit about him. After all, he was my birth father.

She instantly responded that Margaret was not ready to disclose this information, and that she had seemed quite hesitant to give Mary any information relating directly to him. This made me think he and his family might still have some sort of a hold on her. She seemed terrified of people in her area finding out about me – to be almost scared of his family, to this day. After all, he died years ago, and she still will not divulge his name or place of birth. To me she sounded like one frightened lady. I kept making up stories in my head, but I accepted that the truth would probably turn out to have been nothing so dramatic. (The mind can wander off in all directions!)

As I wrote later: *Of course, underneath all this analysis is a feeling that Margaret might not ever want to meet me, unless she can find enough strength to tell her husband and son about my two brothers and me. If she decides against me, I'm not sure how I will deal with the rejection after all the hard work I put into finding her. It would be rejection for a second time, after all, and one doubly hard to take.*

Chapter 28

I woke up on July 7th, 2016 and decided to send the photographs Margaret had requested to Mary. First, I had to have the photographs printed off my phone. These were the old photos my sister sent to me, via text, along with a couple of more recent ones of me. (I made sure my husband and son weren't included in these, of course.)

I sent six photographs altogether, in a card, including a short explanation of each photo. It felt utterly surreal, doing this, almost like an out-of-body experience. I could not get my head around the fact I was posting photographs of myself as a baby to my biological mother. I also had a very strange feeling, which was that Margaret wouldn't want to meet after she received these. We knew that she was already struggling to tell her husband and I worried that the photographs might just be enough to satisfy her maternal instinct. I mentioned this fear to my sister, and she agreed with me. It was already quite a lot for someone to deal with, having Mary suddenly show up with news of me after so many years. It would be still more traumatic to be obliged to tell one's husband about having previously giving away three babies and having kept such a secret from him throughout their married life.

I also feared that this exchange of photographs might prove to be the end of the correspondence – but I hoped that Margaret could find a way to deal with her demons and we could finally start getting to know each other at last.

On July 11th, I phoned Mary to let her know that I had posted the photographs to her, to be forwarded to Margaret. I also asked her if she could post the photograph Margaret had given her for me to my mum's house in Ireland, as we were going there shortly.

However, once Mary responded I was back on the emotional rollercoaster once again.

As I wrote: *Mary has yet again been talking to Margaret and it appears that she has changed her mind and cannot meet me, even though she really wants to. As mentioned earlier, she is frightened of being left alone in her old age. She's also terrified that her husband and son will disown her, and that she might even lose contact with her son, daughter-in-law and grandchildren. Mary apparently suggested that we could meet up, after her second grandchild is born, around the end of July. However, Margaret feels that too much is going on in her life; she "can't think straight". Instead, she has asked that I give her time – to let her get the birth of her new grandchild out of the way, at least. Apparently, Margaret is still considering meeting me on a one-off basis, but we would have to find a neutral place where there was no possibility of her being recognised as she now doubts that she would ever be able to tell her husband about me.*

I felt very worried about these fluctuations in moods and feelings. One-minute Margaret was saying that she couldn't meet me at all – next she was saying maybe we could have a one-off meeting – then she was asking for time. I also felt extremely nervous about the notion of having just a single meeting. I believed that it would be too difficult for me, partly because I'd been through so much over the last two years trying to find her. It would be both too little and too much!

I discussed all this with Max. I felt sad, hurt and even angered by my birth mother's decision. I even felt that she was rejecting me for a second time. However, I was trying to stay strong for Alex. I hadn't told him about the most recent developments and that he might never be able to meet his blood relations.

As I told my husband, there were so many nights as a little girl when I had cried myself to sleep wondering where my mum was and why she had given me away. I'd used to make up fantasies in my head that she was someone famous and had a glamorous life. I had always thought about her on my birthday and wondered if she might be thinking of me. I'd used to cry myself to sleep singing "Nobody's Child". I wasn't sure how many more times I could take these knock-backs. It seemed that every time I imagined that I was getting somewhere, I got knocked back again – this time by my mother herself.

Margaret was apparently holding back on the photograph of herself with my birth father because she feared that local people might recognise her if I ever went looking for her in her hometown. She didn't want to lose the respect she has gained over the past thirty or so years. She didn't want anyone finding out about her past. This was so difficult for me to take in. If I could just have the photograph, I could at least put faces to my biological parents after 47 years! – but it seemed that even the photo would be denied to me.

If she did make the decision never to see me, it would be very difficult for me to deal with, but I would have to respect her decision. She had built a good life for herself and was loved and respected by friends and family. I couldn't face being the cause of her losing all of that. I have asked Mary to hold on to the photographs and not to pass them on. Not yet anyway.

Upon waking on the 13th of July, I felt very sad, very flat – and very down. I couldn't see myself ever meeting Margaret – something very hard to comprehend. I felt like some dirty secret she wanted to keep hidden, an embarrassment. I felt that my existence had only brought shame on her and that I was considered unworthy of even being mentioned to the people dearest to her. I also didn't think that she would ever give me the information I craved.

Mary emailed that afternoon, to ask if we might be able to meet while I was over in Ireland on our week's holiday. I refused, as our week was already so busy. I asked if she had any new information for me. She hadn't. All she had wanted to do was to go through everything with me and to see if I was okay. (Yes: another counselling session.) She had sensed that I was disappointed after what had happened the previous day. I admitted to being extremely disappointed, but I believed that there was nothing to be done. It was Margaret's decision and I had to respect that.

Mary asked me to give it time. She felt that, with time and patience, Margaret would come around. Apparently, she kept saying that she really wanted to meet me but that her "circumstances" would not allow it. I told Mary – as before – that I understood where Margaret was coming from and that I was willing to give her all the time she needed. Mary told me that she would next contact Margaret mid-August. That would give her time to think about things and – maybe – during that time she might even make the decision to tell her husband.

Somehow, though, I didn't think that she would.

Chapter 29

August 8th, 2016.

I spoke to Mary today. It has been nearly a month since I last contacted her. Below is the email from Mary explaining the mind-set of my birth mother. I totally understand how she is feeling. This is a major event in her life, and we may not get the happy ending we all crave.

Hi Alice,

Yes, I made contact with Margaret today. She asks that you give her time, maybe up to six months as she needs time to get her head around all of this as the implications of her telling her story are huge for her and for her future with her husband and son. This makes her very afraid and anxious. She has said however that she will meet you, that she would love to meet you and that she does not wish you to think she is letting you down.

I will be visiting Margaret before the end of the month. I need however to take things very gently with her, given her age and health as I can hear her feelings and what she is telling me very clearly. I fully understand this is very difficult for you and hope you can be patient with Margaret's wishes. She is not closing the door, Alice: she's just asking for more time.

Kind regards

Mary

August 17th.

I had a text from Mary on August 11th. This was very unusual, as she never texts me. The text mentioned that she has been very busy and that she would phone me today, August 17th. She didn't phone. Instead, I ended up phoning her at the end of the day. I was a bit anxious – I thought she had some new information for me. It turned out she hadn't.

Mary really needed to think about how she corresponded with me. On several other occasions she had said she would phone or email me and hadn't, leaving me worrying that something might be seriously wrong, when really there was nothing to report. She didn't take my feelings or state of mind sufficiently into consideration.

Margaret still hadn't changed her mind and was still living in fear of her secret getting out. She was very talkative to Mary when she phoned, though. I thought *Maybe she will come around; with all the counselling she is getting.* I kept coming back to the fact that it wasn't only me; she'd also given up my two brothers for adoption – and her husband didn't know anything about them. I needed to be patient with a capital P.

I had so many questions about my birth father! – but Margaret still refused to release any photos of him. She seemed terrified of him being identified and of people finding out about me. She apparently also still feared that I might take steps to trace his family.

I couldn't help wondering. *What hold did he still have on her? Why had she stayed with him for so long, long enough to have three babies with him? Why had she been with him from such a young age? And what had he done to make her fear him – even long after his death?*

August 23rd

I had a phone call today from Mary, who met Margaret yesterday in her home and who apparently had a two-and-a-half hour counselling session with her.

Amazingly, she said Margaret seemed to be dealing with this upheaval in her life a little better – though she still hadn't told her husband and is still requesting more time. She asked if I could give her the winter, to work up enough courage to tell him. Of course, I said yes. She could have all the time she needs.

Mary took two photographs of Margaret, asking if she could send them to me. And she agreed! They were sent on the condition that I allowed Mary to send the card and my photographs to Margaret in return. I received the photos on my phone. I do not look anything like my birth mother! – I felt a little disappointed, as I had hoped there might be some resemblance. She also looked sad and frail, as if she were carrying the weight of the world on her shoulders. I supposed my sudden reappearance might well have taken a toll on her.

However, Mary also said that Margaret has written me a letter, which she will post on to me. Fantastic news!

I asked her again if Margaret had mentioned my two brothers – but she seemed to think that Margaret had blocked out the fact that they had ever existed. Mary believed that my birth father might have been some sort of control freak when it came to Margaret. He had even asked Margaret if he was the father of my brothers and hadn't believed her when she'd said he was! (She has assured Mary that she had only ever been with him and with her husband.) God only knows what he had said after I was born! – Reading between the lines, I don't think he was a very nice person. I suspect he controlled her; and Mary kept saying that she didn't really like to talk about him. I wondered if it brought back too many bad memories. (Margaret also told Mary, when discussing him, that she "refused to speak ill of the dead".)

Margaret reiterated that she really wanted to meet me because I was her daughter, her first-born. She was simply trying to pluck up enough courage to tell her husband. And, in the meantime, she was willing to correspond, via letters.

That was such good news! – I couldn't wait to receive her first letter!

As I wrote a few days later:

Today is August 27th. I received the letter today. It was short and basic, with only general information. I have to remember that Mary reads all of our correspondence before we receive it. So, we must be careful what we write. Mary also cautioned that, for the first letter, we need to make sure we don't put anything in it that is identifying to ourselves or family members. For example, full names and addresses. Below is a copy.

Dear Evelyn,

So glad to have [redacted] letter and to know you [redacted] been good & had loving parents. Was always thinking about you & hoped that one day we would find each other. Thank you so much for finding me & hope to meet you in the future. Please give me some time to sort out family matters. Any more letters from you would be very welcome. Delighted to hear you are happily married with a little boy. I have one son + 2 grandchildren. I love reading & doing crosswords. I go walking every day with my dog Lucky. My health is fine. Just blood pressure. Ann has a photo for you. Looking forward to one of you.

> you are probably busy getting
> your son back to school. looking
> forward to hearing from you again
> & we will meet up when the time
> is right.
>
> Regards,
> Betty. xxx

It seemed obvious to me that, though she was happy that I'd found her, she was also a little overwhelmed by this major event in her life. She must have a river of emotions running through her! But only two days later, I wrote jubilantly:

August 29th

I hope you are sitting down as I have some fantastic news! Mary called me this afternoon. She said Margaret wants to meet me. OMG! Can you believe it? I can't. I am in shock. What a turnaround. What a change of events.

Margaret received my letter with the photographs on August 26th. She thought I was beautiful. (I'm not really beautiful, of course, but it was nice to hear!)

She finally blurted out to her husband that I had found her!

It turns out that, ever since Margaret first received the letter from Mary – back in June – Margaret's husband had sensed that there was something on her mind. He kept asking her what was bothering her. He even said he had often wondered when I would come knocking on their door! Margaret has showed him the photographs of me. He also said he thought I was beautiful, and that he was happy for her. He even told her that he would be happy for all of us to meet up. He is being very supportive. Wow! Margaret's panic and anxiety were all for nothing!

However, Margaret has only told him about me, not about my brothers; I doubt that she will ever tell him about them. She doesn't talk about them to Mary and she didn't mention them in her letter to me. Mary did say that both boys were taken from her straightaway after giving birth. (I can understand why the youngest boy was because he was adopted privately; I am not sure what happened to the other baby. I am not allowed to know.)

Margaret also gave Mary some information about her youngest son, my half-brother. He is married to a wealthy Italian woman, and they are intensely religious – Orthodox Catholic, if there is such a thing. I don't believe my half-brother will ever know about me and his two half-brothers: Margaret probably wouldn't be able to handle the shame if her secrets were to come out. Yet, to my mind, she had nothing to be ashamed of. She only did what she felt was right for us. . . Well, it worked out for me: I couldn't answer for my brothers.

Margaret wanted to meet in a private place, a place where there was no chance of her being recognised. I suggested Dublin, as I wanted Max to be with me: we could do a day-trip to Dublin. I knew it wasn't ideal for Margaret, but she agreed to meet in Dublin. Fantastic!

Mary told me that Margaret seemed to be opening up more during their counselling sessions, though she still didn't talk about the two boys much. She just said that they had been taken away immediately. Mary mentioned – to me, presumably not to Margaret – that, in some cases, if the nuns thought that the women were suffering, the babies were taken away and the women were told to try to pretend that their baby had died. How inhumane!

As I wrote that evening:

Since I found out – on the 1st of June 2016 – that Margaret was still alive I've been feeling a lot lighter. I feel like I've almost achieved the impossible, because I've had to jump over so many hurdles and was even told, on one occasion, that my mother was dead and – on another – that the social worker and TUSLA had hit a dead end with the search and that I was never going to get anywhere. Sheer determination alone has got me this far. The fact that I found Margaret, despite all the restrictions of the Irish legal system, tells me I can achieve just about anything I put my mind to. The key is to never give up.

Meanwhile, I am gradually starting to feel whole. Eventually, I believe, I will not feel different to other people. My aim is to have some stories, some history, to pass on to my son. After all, it is also a part of his own story.

Throughout my life, I have always cared about what people thought of me. I have always felt that I had to prove myself – especially when I played tennis, in my teens, and, more recently, with my running. When I was younger, I felt I had to prove myself to my adopted dad. I really loved that man. I wanted so desperately for him to be proud of me, and the only way I felt that I could make him proud was to win everything I could. When I came second, I felt I had failed him. The crucial part was this: it wasn't my dad putting me under pressure to win, it was me. I know, deep down, he always was proud of me. It just took me a long time to realise it.

Well, it was all arranged, finally. The date was set for Wednesday, October 5th. On the 27th of September, the week before the big day, I received an email from Mary giving me written directions, the time to meet (no earlier than 11.15, she specified) and her mobile number, in case of emergency. She also attached a document from the Adoption Authority for me to read before meeting Margaret, highlighting areas such as meeting preparation, what my expectations might be, why I wanted the meeting to happen etc. (See appendix).

Chapter 30

The day arrived: an exceedingly early start for us: we were up at 4.45 a.m. (The flight was at 8.00 but we had to be at the airport by 6.30 to allow time to get through security.) As it happened, we had loads of time. Security was easy, and I felt very calm – relaxed even. I don't think it had entirely sunk in why we were at the airport.

We arrived in Dublin Airport at 9 a.m. after an uneventful flight. Max and I made our way out to Heuston Station, on the north side of the city, as Dr Steeven's Hospital was next to it. The bus took us the scenic route, but we still arrived very early, so we decided to have breakfast at the Aisling Hotel, directly opposite the hospital.

Before I knew it, it was 11.15 a.m. and I had started to get quite nervous – though I wasn't sure why, because I hadn't felt worried before. . . Mary had asked me to arrive no earlier than 11:15 because she'd wanted to get Margaret settled and calm before our meeting.

Max and I walked across the road to the hospital, once an Accident and Emergency Hospital but these days only used for administration, and in desperate need of a makeover. As we entered the reception, my heart was hammering. I thought *My birth mother is in the same building!*

When Mary joined us in the reception area, I introduced Max, as they had never met before. Then Max headed back to the Aisling Hotel, where he could nurse a coffee while answering business calls on his mobile. Meanwhile, Mary led me upstairs and along the corridor to the room where Margaret was waiting. I took a deep breath as Mary knocked and then opened the door.

Margaret was clearly very emotional at seeing me. The first thing she said was, as if in disbelief, "She's beautiful!" I smiled back and said "Hello." I started to take my jacket off – it was so hot – but before I knew it, she was hugging me and would not let me go. Sobbing, she seemed overwhelmed. She was also extremely apologetic – she could not stop saying how sorry and guilty she felt about giving me up.

As for me, I just didn't seem to feel anything instinctive towards her. I was secretly surprised because I'd imagined that I would be an emotional wreck. (I am generally quite soft. I cry at the drop of a hat.)

But that day, I felt numbed: I didn't seem to know what to do or what to say, at least at first, when faced with this storm of emotion. Luckily, Mary had remained in the room and she eventually managed to calm Margaret down. (Mary was, I believe, genuinely concerned for Margaret, as she has very high blood pressure.) Mary stayed with us for twenty minutes or so and then asked if we wanted to be left alone, which – by then – we did.

It was hard to ask questions, as I had so many! – and as I didn't want to ask anything that would upset her or bring back too many difficult memories.

Once Margaret had finished apologising, she did mention that she believed that she had been right to give me up for adoption. She had only been twenty; her father had been dying of cancer; she had felt utterly hopeless about the kind of life she could offer me. She had missed me and remembered me and had even considered looking for me – but she hadn't wanted to intrude on my life and spoil things for me. She had also felt that, if I had wanted her in my life, I could have searched for her. (Which I had!)

At first, I was mostly trying to reassure her. I shared tales of my happy upbringing, explaining to her how wonderful my parents had been, both to me and to my adopted brother and sister. How privileged I felt to have been adopted into my family – not just my immediate family but also my extended family. How I had always felt completely accepted. She was so happy to hear that – possibly because her own childhood, as I later learned, had been so different – that she cried again. . . Or possibly she cried because she only knew, in that moment, that she had made the right decision, all those decades ago?

She told me that she'd had such a hard life – as hard a life as I'd feared. After having been abandoned by her birth mother, her own adoptive parents had taken her in. She was never legally adopted, though, as the adoption law in Ireland only came in the early 50s. So, she has always – her whole life – been treated as a second-class citizen.

We spoke a little about my birth father. She admitted to me that she hadn't wanted to paint a bad picture of my birth father to Mary. I immediately assured her, "I want to know the whole truth about him. I'm guessing that you might have had a rough time with him." Mary, who had now returned, supported me, at this point, telling Margaret that I had mentioned to her my suspicion that she had endured a great deal.

Margaret finally surrendered and told me some facts about my birth father and their situation. (I cannot even honestly call it a relationship because I do not believe there was one.) Briefly, my birth father was apparently a controlling, manipulative and domineering man who had taken advantage of an innocent, vulnerable young girl, who had suffered from exceptionally low self-esteem. I could completely understand why she had previously tried to avoid talking about him.

I also believe that recalling my birth father brought back a lot of painful memories. She tried to describe him but could not seem to get the words out, so Mary interrupted – very uncharacteristically – saying, "He was a predator." Margaret looked quite shocked but then nodded in agreement. After a while, presumably upon reflection, Mary apologised for using the word. (Even though I believed it to have been completely correct, and so – I suspected – did Margaret herself.)

My birth father had groomed her for sex from the age of fifteen – even before she had started having her periods. Basically, it was child abuse. Unfortunately, Margaret hadn't known any better. She had never been told about the birds and the bees. She hadn't even known what her periods were about! – I also think she was longing to feel loved. (After all, she had been abandoned by her birth mother.) My birth father had also bought her gifts. He'd thrown a 21st birthday party for her, two months after she'd given me away. He had even bought her a gold bracelet – which she has since given to me.

But all the time he was showering her with gifts he had numerous other women on the go (though probably not all as young as fifteen.) He had used, controlled and groomed her for many years. He had even dictated whom she could – and could not – meet! – He seemed to have perceived her almost as his property, even though he put on a pretence that they were in a loving relationship – something which Margaret had been innocent enough to believe. Even her own adoptive mother had been fooled: to her, my birth father could do no wrong. Margaret told me his name: Peter. (She would only tell me his first name.)

When Margaret went into labour prematurely with me, as we knew, Peter had been playing snooker in the church hall with the parish priest. What she hadn't confessed before was that she'd been obliged to wait until he'd finished the match before he could be bothered to get her to Sean Ross Abbey. And, after she delivered me, he actually told her to get rid of the baby! (Apparently, his parents also didn't want anything to do with me, though that might have been shame.)

I'd already been told that, upon Margaret's entering the Abbey, Peter had paid the nuns £100 so Margaret could be a private patient. What I hadn't known: Peter had also bribed the nuns, so that she could leave Sean Ross Abbey as soon as possible after the birth. I had weighed only 4 pounds and 4 ounces at birth, and I could not be legally adopted until I reached at least 5lbs. I reached this weight after only three weeks! Margaret said Peter had been so desperate to get her out of Sean Ross Abbey that he had paid the nuns extra to speed up the adoption process. Her words were stark: "There were lots of brown envelopes being passed under the table".

I believed that Peter might have also paid the St Claire nuns, in Stamullen, but I had no way of proving this, of course, because Peter was no longer alive.

Do you remember back when I asked Mary to check out whether my adoptive dad had given monetary donations to the nuns in Stamullen? – Well, I now doubt that he'd needed to: my birth father had paid them quite enough, all on his own! Margaret had been utterly astonished at how quickly my adoption had happened: women were generally in the laundries for six to twelve months before a home was found for their babies. I was adopted after only three weeks.

So, Margaret had been free to leave. But she had still faced verbal abuse and condescension and been viewed as totally at fault. Her confidence back then, by her own admission, had been almost non-existent. Yet Peter had continued to control and manipulate her for years afterwards, resulting in two more babies given up for adoption. (She confirmed to me that these two boys are indeed my full brothers.)

As we knew, one boy was born in Limerick hospital – but the other was born in Portlaoise, as Sean Ross Abbey was closed by 1974. (Another piece of false information from TUSLA!) Peter had arranged, in both cases, for the nurses to take them away from Margaret immediately. He had wanted to get rid of them, just as he had wanted to be rid of me. Thanks to him, poor Margaret never even saw my two brothers.

As if all this wasn't bad enough, Peter had also accused Margaret of sleeping with other men, claiming, wrongly, that he wasn't the father of my brothers. Also, after she had me (but before she had my brothers) he kept assuring her that she would not get pregnant again. I asked her if he had stayed away from her over the five years before my brother Patrick was born. She said simply, "No, not at all, I just got lucky." He had controlled her utterly: she had believed every word he said.

By this point I understood why Mary, normally so discreet, had described him as a predator. What a monster! – and Margaret hadn't even been the only young woman he was grooming. He had been seeing several other young women at the same time. (Who knows how many half-siblings of mine he might have been responsible for?)

Margaret finally escaped from Peter once she managed to save up enough money to buy herself a car. At that time, she had been caring for her elderly mother and had depended on Peter to take her grocery shopping. That was the biggest hold he'd had over her but – once she had her own car – she no longer needed him for anything. She had won her independence, along with a little confidence and dignity at last. At that point she met Jack, to whom she has been happily married to for thirty-six years. Unbelievably, when their relationship first started Peter had tried to split them up, even though he no longer wanted a sexual relationship with her. No: if he could not have her, no one could else could!

The bottom line about my birth father's attitude was: he used Margaret only for sex, and he treated her with no respect. He didn't want anyone to know about the children he'd pressured her to give away because he perceived her as a second-class citizen. When he took Margaret to Sean Ross Abbey, he left her there to return to his snooker!

Margaret didn't go into any detail about her time in Sean Ross Abbey, or about her birthing experience, either. Perhaps she couldn't – or didn't want to – remember. She did recall being taken there, and she vividly remembered not being allowed to hold me or to feed me.

She also remembered Sister Hildegarde and Sister Frances: the nuns depicted in the film *Philomena.* Sister Hildegarde, particularly, seemed to have been a horrible person. Margaret observed a lot of cruelty and abuse towards the other unmarried mothers, but she didn't experience any herself – presumably as she was a private patient. I suppose the nuns were careful how they treated her – since Peter was handing over brown envelopes as if they were going out of fashion!

The impression I received was that she didn't want to go into much detail as it would have brought back bad memories – not only of being in Sean Ross Abbey but of the time she spent with Peter and of the humiliating abuse she suffered. Young and innocent as she had been, she cannot be held to blame for anything that happened. I blame Peter for being a predator – but I also blame the social norms of the time – and the Church itself – for turning a blind eye to all those unfortunate women.

Yet I was surprised at how I felt towards Margaret. She honestly felt like a stranger to me. I really didn't feel anything *terribly personal* towards her at all – I felt great compassion for what she'd been through, but much less emotional than I'd expected.

Margaret and I spent two hours talking in the little room in that outdated hospital. I was feeling intensely grateful to her, but still was rather relieved when the meeting ended, as I was worn out. Once Mary finally returned, we all left together. (Before we met each other's husbands, Margaret reminded me not to mention my two brothers, as Jack "didn't know about them" – which I already knew, of course, from Mary. In that moment I heard the nervousness in her tone, and sensed something of the panic she felt, in case her secret somehow slipped out.)

I introduced Max to Margaret, and then we all walked across to Heuston Station to meet Jack: a lovely man who seemed very supportive to Margaret.

We all exchanged phone numbers. But once we were alone, I turned to Max, saying, "I am glad that we met, but I don't want to have a relationship with her. She brought me into this world, and I will always be grateful to her – but I don't feel anything towards her as a person . . .That sounds cold-hearted, but it's simply the way I feel. I will need to let her down gently, as I get the impression that she wants to form a relationship with me, but we lead such different lives. We have nothing in common – we don't even look alike!"

Max listened and listened – he's the most wonderfully sympathetic listener – but I think the truth was, every time I thought about her and all she had been through, I also remembered Peter, the type of man he was and what he did to her – and I couldn't "own" that.

During our two-hour conversation, Margaret had given me several photographs of Peter – but I found that I couldn't even bear to look at them. I'd have been far happier burning them, as – after all Margaret had shared, the thought of him disgusted me. I couldn't see any resemblance to me in either of my parents – though I must admit to wondering if I looked anything like my brothers. (I do not resemble my half-brother, who is very like Margaret's husband.)

I kept thinking about how different Peter had been to my adoptive father! I could not have asked or wished for a better dad. My father had been one in a million, one of the kindest, best liked and most generous men I've ever known. I was the luckiest baby girl in Ireland to have had him choose me!

I supposed I should be thankful that Peter generally enjoyed good health. Margaret, however, suffers from high blood pressure so I need to tread carefully. When I told Max this, he said that I needed to do whatever felt right for me, adding reassuringly, "You're nothing like either of them. You're your own person." (It is – thankfully – all down to my upbringing, and to the family and friends that surrounded me that he was right about this.)

Later, as we walked around Dublin that beautiful autumn day, I couldn't help absurdly grinning to myself. I felt truly relieved to have been on this journey and to have come out on the other side: I had a great sense of achievement. I felt uplifted and glad that I had found my birth mother – despite all the obstacles – and to have had so many questions answered at last.

The gap in my history had been filled. I felt 100% whole, for first time ever.

My background had always been felt as a nagging worry in the back of my mind. It felt so good to know who I was, and where I had come from, in the deepest sense – and, even if some of it had been painful – it was such a gift!

Max and I enjoyed a lovely afternoon in Dublin before heading out to the airport for the evening flight. The airport was quiet for a Wednesday evening and we wandered into the bar and had a couple of glasses of wine before our flight. (Well, I had the wine as Max had to drive us home when we landed.) I also typed up my notes from the day as I wanted to do it while everything was fresh in my mind. Max was shattered: he fell asleep as I texted Alex, making sure he was okay and looking after our dog.

We arrived home late: the plane had been parked on the Manchester runway for quite a while, without explanation. At 10.30 Alex was still awake, and curious about everything that had happened. I told him briefly what had happened, promising to tell him the rest in the morning. As I wrote the following day:

I couldn't sleep last night: my mind was working overtime. I kept going over and over the meeting in my head, thinking about everything that was said. I tossed and turned all night, and this morning I felt completely drained. I told Max I couldn't work: I was just too tired to concentrate. I got to see Alex before he went to school, then I crawled back to bed.

Later I decided to check Facebook, only to discover that Margaret had sent me a friend request, which I neither accepted nor declined. The reasons being, first: I don't want her to see and know every aspect of my life. I am just not ready for that. And second, she seems to be quite excited about forming a relationship: to her, I'm the long-lost daughter she gave away.

But for me, right now, it's really more about having my questions answered and filling the void. I have gone to a lot of trouble to find her. She has apologised for giving me away and I think she feels all is forgiven. She has her daughter back. But, really, there was nothing to forgive – I don't hold it against her for giving me away. In fact, I am intensely grateful to her!

Don't get me wrong, I'm very glad I found her, but I didn't go through all this to play Happy Families. At the end of the day this woman is still a stranger. I don't want to form a relationship with her, just at the minute. She needed time before – well, now it's me needing more time and to keep a little distance between us. Perhaps I'm being selfish – when she has answered so many of the questions I've been wondering about for years – but in a way she has bridged the gap, so that I can close this chapter in my life and move on.

Given time I may change my mind. I will just have to wait and see.

Chapter 31

After that day in Dublin, and after finding out exactly what type of man my birth father had been, I asked Mary to find out from Margaret if she had ever feared for me with Peter around. I wondered if this might have been another reason why she gave me away.

Hi Mary,

Did you manage to speak to Margaret? How is she? I'm still trying to get my head around my birth father and what he was like. I know you can't break any confidences, but do you think she feared for me being around him? Could that have been part of the reason she gave me away? Also: did he physically abuse her? Is there anything else you can tell me about their relationship? I'm not at home today but if you could email me back that would be great. Mentally, I am fine so don't worry about me needing counselling. I have been talking to my counsellor friend this morning.

Alice

Hi Alice,

I managed to speak to Margaret yesterday. She was very tired and puts this down to processing all the resurrected feelings which are coming up for her on an ongoing basis around being searched for etc. I think that I mentioned before that her main reason for placing you for adoption was that her father, who was dying from cancer at the time, was so ill that she felt it would put too much pressure on both her parents to bring you home. Reflecting on this, it would appear she was in the middle of a terrible grief, complicated with guilt and shame about her own situation, for her father whom she loved dearly.

She told me your birth father did not physically abuse her. She explained that the relationship was built on pure control and attributes her part in it to her lack of confidence, based on herself being an adopted child and being raised where the whole community knew her story and shamed her during her childhood and adolescent years. I hope I am painting a picture to you of a very disempowered young girl who went into labour not knowing what was happening, or even that she was only 32 weeks pregnant.

I know this is all very difficult information for you and I am glad you are in touch with your counsellor friend. We just have to remember that she stands to lose an awful lot and we need to be very tender with her about her situation. I hope you also will take time to process the feelings in relation to your sense of identity etc. and that you will take things slowly and gently from here.

Take care.

Kind regards

Mary

Chapter 32

We are into January 2017: and I have wound up visiting Ireland three times within five weeks!

Firstly, my mum fell extremely ill with pneumonia and was in hospital for a week. She was then transferred to a nursing home for a fortnight. I travelled to Ireland to spend some time with her when she came out of the nursing home.

When I first saw her afterwards, I couldn't believe my eyes. She seemed to have become so frail and weak – she had also lost a lot of weight – weight she could ill-afford to lose. She suddenly looked every bit her eighty-six years. I stayed with her for a few days to make sure she was eating properly and was gaining some strength before flying back to the UK on October 3rd.

Two days later, October 5th, Max and I flew back to Dublin to meet Margaret for the first time, as described above.

And then, only four weeks later, on November 4th, I got a call from my mum to say my aunt had passed away: she had suffered a brain haemorrhage whilst walking up the stairs. My mum was devastated. Of course, I had to fly back to Ireland for the funeral, and to be with my mum.

It was a well-attended and very sorrowful funeral, as my late aunt had been very popular and loved by everyone. It was heart breaking to see the devastation that her sudden death had caused. There were hordes of people at the graveside – even though it was freezing, and I feared that my mother might suffer a relapse. But there was no talking to her: she absolutely insisted upon being there for her sister. After staying with her for a couple of days, I flew back to England.

Being in Ireland, especially under those circumstances, helped me to do a lot of thinking. Thinking about life in general and how short it can be.

When I first started compiling this book, I only planned a memoir, in diary form, for Alex to read once he was older. I wanted to share everything I had learned about myself and his birth grandparents with him. I wanted him to see that the information he has always known about himself – about his birth – did not come so easily to me. I have had to fight tooth and nail for my information and I'm still chasing it, through Margaret. I also wanted it all to be written down so that he could refer to it – or perhaps to choose to share it with his own children someday.

But since writing it, I now hope to publish it so that anyone interested can understand the difficulties I endured in gaining this precious data but also to help other people who are in a similar situation get their valuable information.

I have also started to do a lot of thinking about Margaret and about all she had to cope with when she was young. I have started to wonder again about Peter and Margaret and their relationship. About the way Margaret was treated by Peter, by his family and – perhaps especially – by her community. Recent events had shown me that life is too short – my aunt died walking up the stairs! – so I needed to act now and ask the questions I still desperately wanted answers for . . . Even though I was unsure if those questions would ever be answered, as Margaret was not replying to my texts and had not responded to my recent letter.

Below is an extract:

Dear Margaret,

I do hope this letter finds you in good health. When I spoke to Mary a few weeks ago she said your blood pressure was a bit on the high side. I hope it's all under control now.

I also hope all is well with Jack, your son and his family. No doubt your granddaughter is excited about Christmas.

Margaret, I'm not sure how you feel about us keeping in touch after our initial meeting. Would you like us to stay in contact? If you prefer, we could stay in touch by letter or, if you have an email address, we could correspond that way. It's entirely up to you.

I've been doing a lot of thinking about you and Peter and I would like to know more about both of you. If you did mention his last name to me then it has completely slipped my memory: I think we were both in shock that day in Dublin! If you could tell me a bit more about Peter and his family, I would be grateful. Also, a bit more detail about yourself. About your adopted parents, your childhood, your birth parents and how you and Peter met.

I would like to know in more detail about the day both of you took me to Dublin. What you were wearing? The model of car Peter was driving? I do understand it might be difficult for you to remember, but it might help me get to know him and the type of person he was. And also, the trauma you had to deal with. Writing this down might help you. You might feel lighter, that a burden had been lifted. I do hope I am not asking too much.

I do hope you understand why I'm keen to know about you and your past. To me all of this is also a part of me and my history.

I would like for us to keep in contact. I do realise that we both need time to come to terms with recent events. You can text me anytime or, if you prefer, write me a letter or email.

I also sent a text to Margaret, asking her if she had received the letter and if she would like to stay in contact. (No reply.)

I feared that she was distancing herself, as she was still so frightened that her secrets might be revealed. I also worried that she might never open up to me – even though Mary had assured me that I could text and ask Margaret questions at any time.

I decided to leave it and to await a response. My gut feeling was that I might never hear from her again. I hoped that, over time, she would communicate with me – but potentially – she still had a lot to lose.

Chapter 33

I am sitting here in my living room typing away on my iPad. It is a freezing cold January day. I am sitting in front of the wood-burning stove obsessively watching my messages as they come in, to see if any are from Margaret.

I haven't received any yet. She is ignoring my last text.

As I write this, my uncle, my mum's brother, is dying in a hospital in Ireland. I dread to think what she must be feeling, losing another sibling so soon. It has been said that he might not survive the week. Of course, I will have to go to Ireland for the funeral.

My uncle passed away on Monday 16th January 2017. This was devastating for my mum, who had buried her sister only nine weeks before.

I travelled to Ireland two days later, to be with my mum, who was heartbroken. My cousins travelled from America to say farewell to their beloved father. It was altogether a very sad occasion.

After the funeral, family, friends, and people who had travelled a distance to the funeral were invited to the local pub, for refreshments and a hot meal. As day slipped into evening and people relaxed, a group of us cousins were chatting and telling stories about our childhoods, and about our fond memories of those of our aunts and uncles who have now died.

During this reminiscing session we managed to get onto the topic of godparents. My cousin turned to me and asked me who my godparents were. I replied by saying, "I don't have any godparents". She gave a little nervous laugh and said, "You must do!" At this point another cousin added, "Of course you have godparents – everyone does." Then my sister stepped in and backed me up: neither of us had godparents, of course, even though our cousins had automatically assumed we had. That it was a given. Then, they asked if I was baptised. To which I replied "Yes, I was baptised in Sean Ross Abbey before Mum and Dad got me."

My cousins looked at me, astonished. Then I looked at my sister and asked, 'Do you think that this is the right time to tell them my story?" She thought it was. So, I asked them to be quiet just for a little while as I told them: about my search for Margaret, the difficulties I endured, our meeting, and how I'd finally managed to get some questions answered. They were so happy for me! I also told them that, for me, nothing has changed. I still feel a part of the family. I may not have the family blood, but I still have the family name.

Then my cousin turned to me and said, "You always were and always will be part of this family. Blood doesn't come into it."

Those words meant so much to me!

My cousins were particularly appalled to hear about the discrimination that Margaret had suffered, and what she had seen others suffer at the hands of the nuns in Sean Ross Abbey. They could hardly believe that nuns could do such things, and, of course, they seemed shocked to hear that I had been born in such a dreadful place. I told them about Margaret's delivering me and not being allowed to hold me, about her having to express milk so the nuns could bottle-feed me, and about Margaret's having to hold me on that long journey to Dublin – only to have to hand me over to the nuns under Clerys clock.

I also told them about Peter. How he had manipulated her from such a noticeably young age. How he controlled every aspect of her life. How he grilled her about his being the father of my younger brothers. They could not believe how desperate Peter was to get rid of me by handing over the brown envelopes to the nuns – but they were even more shocked by the greed of the nuns.

None of my cousins could understand how the authorities could put so many obstacles in my way. How they messed up the search on two occasions. They couldn't believe it when I admitted that a team leader told me to accept the information I was given was correct or else they would stop the search – even though I knew that they'd got hold of the wrong person. I could see the disbelief and horror etched on their faces as I told my story. They had loads of questions! – naturally, they would have heard and read about stories like mine but the fact that this had occurred in their own family circle hit them hard.

I felt a sense of catharsis telling my story, and I felt proud of myself for having taken on this journey. I knew that it wasn't a fairy-tale ending – but at least I could now own my beginnings. I also felt that the journey itself had changed me: I had a lot more self-confidence. I felt that I could do just about anything I put my mind to.

That was a really good feeling.

Chapter 34

It was February 2017 and I still hadn't heard from Margaret. I was starting to get a bit worried, so I decided to email Mary to see if she had heard anything. I explained that I had sent a letter and two texts to Margaret without a response and that I was starting to worry about her. I was wondering if she had heard from Margaret and if she was in good health. I got this terse reply: "Best if you call me".

Below are exact copies of the emails:

Hi Mary,

Hope all is well with you. Just wondering if you have heard from Margaret lately? I sent her a letter in December and a couple of texts after Christmas but haven't heard from her. Do you know if she is okay? Or if she's receiving my texts?

Alice

Hi Alice,

Best if you call me.

Mary

Imagine what was going through my mind. I was thinking the worst. These emails were sent at 10.45 a.m.: I eventually got to speak to her at 3.30. Mary admitted that she hadn't heard from Margaret since before Christmas. She did say that Margaret was still traumatised and was struggling to come to terms with recent events. My finding her had been a massive life event for her to deal with. She was still living in fear of her son, my half-brother, finding out about me – as well as her husband finding out about the two boys. She was probably still terrified that they might disown her and leave her all alone in her old age. We three are the age-old dirty secrets, after all.

But Mary also said: "You did ask her questions, in your letter, about the day she took you to Dublin and also about your birth father's full name, didn't you?"

Now, how could Mary have known these things if she hadn't heard from Margaret? My gut feeling – amounting to a near-certainty – is that she opened my sealed letter, and read it before posting it on to my birth mother . . . She was practically repeating the wording in my letter, word for word.

I was furious about this. I had been assured, before sending the letter, that it would be forwarded on to Margaret and wouldn't be tampered with. Also, Mary had asked me recently if I was writing a book. That people in my situation generally do. I strongly suspected that she had warned Margaret about the possibility of my writing a book. This revelation could well have made Margaret even more scared and paranoid about her secrets than she had been already. She was keeping her distance – and not responding to my letter or texts – perhaps for that reason alone!

In my opinion Mary – assuming I was correct – had acted considerably outside her remit. What gave her the right to read that private and confidential letter? – let alone to pass it on? Nothing. She had no such right.

This is what I have had to deal with, over and over, during the past few years! The social workers always need to be in control, and Mary – especially – tended to get involved without due cause. I had written a private letter, addressed to Margaret, assuming that only Margaret would receive it. Mary had no right to interfere, potentially putting the fear of God into Margaret.

By doing this, Mary has made it more difficult for Margaret and me to form a relationship. She has put doubts in Margaret's mind about my motives and about whether she could really trust me. To put it bluntly: She has betrayed my trust in her and undermined Margaret's trust in me.

Chapter 35

October 25th, 2016:

I have decided to concentrate on finding my siblings, both brothers. (I still find it hard to believe, after all these years, I have two full brothers!)

And on this point, I have exciting news, which is that the social worker dealing with tracing my siblings has been in touch today. (I should mention that this social worker is not the same as the one who dealt with tracing my birth mother. I am pleased about that because, as you might have guessed, I am not overly impressed with how the search for my birth mother was handled.)

This new social worker, Ben, was from the Adoption Authority. Ben was very pleasant, easy to talk to and approachable. He did not speak to me in a patronising manner and he genuinely seemed to want to help. He did not appear to be putting obstacles in my way. As I wrote: *I hope I am still singing his praises by the time I finish this book!*

You may remember, back in April 2016, that I had received a phone call from Ben saying that there had been a match for me and a sibling on the contact register. My (second) brother had registered on the National Preference Contact Register, back in 2005, when it was first set up. Ben had written letters to the address on the Register and also made phone calls to the landline number – but without success. Ben had also asked the Department for Social Protection to write a letter on his behalf: still no response. I had spoken to Ben recently about my brother, but he hadn't anything new to tell me. I asked if it were possible that he could be in prison. Ben said that it was a possibility, but that the prison service generally refused to release the identities of those serving a sentence, though he would do what he could to find out.

But there were a few other possibilities. My brother may have emigrated – while keeping his property in Ireland. He may also be dead, though Ben has confirmed that there is no record of his death in the GRO in Dublin.

But there was also another possibility: he might no longer want to be found. Although he had put his name on the Register originally, he might have changed his mind. Some people did.

Below are the emails.

Hi Ben,

Just wondering if you had any luck in tracing my brothers. My birth mother has given permission for all of us siblings to be in contact. So, I would really like to get in touch with both my full brothers, if possible.

Alice

Hello Alice,

As there is still no reply from the gentleman who submitted his details on the National Contact Register, I am giving it one more shot and have requested information from the Dept of Social Protection. They are usually fairly quick about replying so I should know by early next week if they have a place on file to which I can send a letter asking him to contact me. If they have his details, they will forward a letter from me but will not share those details with me: also, if I do get to send a letter, he may or may not reply. I suspect that he has moved from the address he submitted on his registration details and that my letters to date have not been passed on.

I will keep you posted on any developments.

Regards

Ben

But I didn't have to wait long before penning this in the diary:

Exciting news! Ben emailed to let me know he managed to track down my other brother, the baby born in 1974. Wow! What a result! Below is the email.

25/10/2016

Hi Alice,

Sorry for not getting back sooner but there has been a development in the trace.

Yesterday I met with a gentleman, the elder of your two brothers, the one born in 1974. It took a long time to confirm his identity and get contact details, which is why I have had nothing to update you on till now. Unfortunately, there is still no contact from the younger brother, born in 1975.

This gentleman knew nothing of his adoption until he was in late primary school. His father has been dead for many years and his mother (now in her 80s) has early-onset dementia and he is not going to address this with her.

He is entirely sympathetic to the fact that a birth family member is looking for information, but he says that he is not ready to engage in this yet. He never thought about tracing his siblings over the years and explained that he needs time to process all of this. He said that he will contact me when he has made a decision, but that this will not be for another six months to a year, at the earliest. I left it open to him to contact me at any stage if he wants to.

We had a long discussion, but I'm not in a position to give any more information without his express permission. Obviously, I will let you know if there are any developments before then.

Regards

Ben

You can only imagine how ecstatic I was feeling! At least one of my brothers had been located – and in Ireland too. It was a start! I only hoped that one day, he would want to meet me. It would be fantastic to meet my full brother after all these years!

During the six months I had been waiting to hear from Ben I'd also been training hard for the Manchester marathon. (I had already run two half-marathons, in April and October 2017.) Training kept my mind clear and positive – so much so that I ran the marathon on the 2nd of April in four hours and thirty-eight minutes, a fantastic achievement for me. I felt stronger mentally when I ran: it cleared my mind and helped me to focus. I was concentrating on training for a half-marathon in May 2017 when it happened.

Fantastic news! Ben phoned this morning, the 6th of March, telling me he spoke to my brother today. My brother's name is Patrick and he is married. At this stage, Ben is not allowed to give me any more information until we have our first meeting. But he told me that Patrick has given our situation a lot of thought and has decided that he wants to meet me.

I still cannot believe it!

While I had Ben's attention, I asked if Patrick knew about Margaret and her circumstances. Below is an email I received from Ben that same day. The email gave me more of a clue as to where Patrick was emotionally.

06/03/2017

Hi Alice,

Patrick doesn't know anything about Margaret. He has not searched for her previously and, until I met him, I don't believe he had thought about doing so. Best not to go into Margaret just yet as contact with you is a big thing for him first.

Margaret is not aware of your finding each other, but this possibility has been addressed with her by Mary and she did not object to you and your brothers finding and having contact with each other.

Regards

Ben

My head was spinning. I could not believe that this was actually happening! – Ben also told me that the next step is for us to exchange letters and a photograph, but not our full names or our addresses. My brother requested that I write first – which Ben thought a good idea, as I've "been here before" – with Margaret. This was all new to Patrick: he might be a bit overwhelmed.

I wrote the letter and posted it the following day, with a photograph enclosed. It took Patrick a whole six weeks to respond. I was very anxious during this time because (of course) I feared he would change his mind about meeting me. I kept in touch with Ben, however, who kept reassuring me that Patrick had not changed his mind. He just did not know how to construct the letter!

Ben phoned Patrick a few times during this period, to make sure that we were still on track. All Patrick could say was, "I have the letter written in my head but I'm not sure how to put it on to paper!" I totally understood where he is coming from. I had also struggled, because we were so restricted in what information we could share. In my letter I had only mentioned being married with a child – and about having enjoyed a happy childhood with a large extended family.

On Thursday April 13th, the day before Good Friday, Ben finally managed to pin down Patrick and (more or less) wrote the letter from him. As I wrote:

At last I got the email with the letter and photograph attached. It feels weird looking at a photograph of my brother. There is some slight resemblance. We have the same smile. (Wow!) Also, he wrote a lovely letter. He had a very similar upbringing to me: he was also adopted into a large extended family. Though he was an only child. I am so pleased he had a happy life with good parents and extended family around him, and that he is married (though without children, but perhaps that might have been a choice?)

The next step is for us to meet. I suggested May, maybe the 10th or 17th. Both dates are convenient for Max and me to travel to Dublin for the day.

I mentioned to Ben that I have some concerns about what I can tell Patrick about Margaret and Peter. I have said all along that, if Patrick asks me about Margaret, I will tell him the truth. I am not prepared to lie to him or to keep any information from him – especially after everything I've been through over the past three years!

Ben assures me that he will speak to Patrick before the meeting and tell him what he can and cannot ask – though I don't think this very fair on Patrick. I feel that, if he wants to know about Margaret, I should be allowed to tell him – at least what I know myself. We are both her children, after all!

Ben has emailed me a couple of times since, mentioning that he met both Patrick and his wife Sarah on the 24th of April. They have agreed to meet Max and me in Dublin on May 10th. I booked the flights immediately after reading Ben's email.

This feels so significant. I am going to meet my full brother, at last!

Chapter 36

The morning of the 10th of May has arrived! Ben phoned yesterday to check that we could still make it to the meeting tomorrow. I told him that we could. I feel very optimistic and excited about the meeting.

Max and I were up at 5a.m., to catch the 8a.m. flight to Dublin. The airport was quiet: the flight took off on time and we landed in Dublin ahead of schedule. On the airport bus to the city centre, the sun was shining, and Dublin looked beautiful.

We managed to find a café off Grafton Street where we could sit outside, have breakfast and watch the world go by. After breakfast we found a bench in St Stephen's Green. . . It was so lovely to sit in the sunshine, away from the hustle and bustle of the city!

After a while we walked to Trinity College and had a look around the centuries-old campus. The meeting wasn't scheduled until one, so Max and I wandered to the Westbury Hotel for coffee before making our way to the offices of the Adoption Authority on Shelborne Road, Ballsbridge.

We arrived early, at Ben's request. Patrick had been asked to arrive at 1.15 p.m. but actually appeared shortly after two: I was beginning to fear that he'd changed his mind!

Max was asked to sit in the next room while Ben and I waited for my brother. When Patrick and his wife Sarah arrived, she joined Max, while Ben escorted Patrick into the room where I was waiting.

My first impression was that Patrick was extremely nervous and jumpy. He gave me a quick hug and sat down opposite me.

It was soon apparent that Patrick knew absolutely nothing of our background – he had so many questions! He didn't have any information at all about Margaret, not even her name. . . Now Ben had mentioned beforehand that I shouldn't give out any identifying information about Margaret. I had agreed – though I felt hypocritical. As mentioned before, I thought that my brother had the right to know everything I did. But I accepted the obligation to protect Margaret, because of her fragile state of mind.

I noticed that Patrick looked a little like Margaret and told him so: then I showed him a photograph of her. He looked a bit taken aback. It must feel so strange, not only to see your birth mother for the first time but also to bear some resemblance to her! – I answered all his questions the best I could, though it got awkward, especially when he asked where Margaret lived, and whether I thought she might like to meet him. I tried to explain Margaret's current circumstances and state of mind. I felt terrible, not only mentioning that she might not want to meet him – at least, not so soon – but also that Margaret's husband still knew nothing, about either Patrick or our brother. I asked him to try to understand how embarrassed and ashamed she felt about having three babies and giving them all away. That was incredibly stressful for us both: I suspected that he was probably feeling rejected for the second time by his birth mother.

I explained that Margaret had endured a very hard life until she'd met Jack – that our birth father had treated her badly. However, I didn't go into any level of detail, because I could see that Patrick was struggling to take everything in. I thought it would be better if we discussed our father some other time.

On a personal level, Patrick and I hit it off straightaway. Ben could see this and after a while we invited Max and Sarah to join us. It felt quite strange sitting in a room with my brother and his wife after all these years! – but it also felt right and comfortable.

During the meeting I asked Ben if Margaret was aware that this meeting was taking place. He was sure that Mary had spoken to Margaret about it. He also asked me to write a letter to Margaret, telling her about my meeting Patrick at last, but I refused, as I felt that I wouldn't be able to live with myself if Jack happened to see the letter. The responsibility just felt too great. Ben instantly saw the justice of this: he agreed to ask Mary to phone Margaret instead.

After the meeting, all four of us headed to a nearby pub for some lunch and a much-needed alcoholic drink. We talked for ages, marvelling that we had grown up only a half-hour's drive away from each other. (We so easily could have met, and never even known that we were related!)

We also talked about keeping in touch. Patrick appeared quite keen. He had grown up believing himself an only child – but now he has a sister. It might take him a little time to get used to that! We all exchanged phone numbers before Patrick and Sarah dropped us at the airport. At the end of the encounter, we hugged and promised to keep in touch. . . The next day we befriended each other on Facebook and agreed to meet in the summer.

My head was buzzing when I got home, but I was too tired to write much. Just: *What a successful day! Today I met my brother!*

Chapter 37

Monday the 15th of May 2017. I first met Patrick last Wednesday, May 10th. Since the meeting I have been thinking a lot about him and Margaret. I have been wondering if Mary has let Margaret know about the latest developments. It has been on my mind all weekend.

This morning I decided to phone Margaret because I felt she has a right to know what is going on. So, I sent her a text to see if it was okay to phone. She said it was. I phoned in the afternoon: she seemed very pleased to hear from me. She was very upbeat and chatty, which was lovely to hear. I asked her if she had heard from Mary regarding the meeting between Patrick and me. She said she hadn't. She wasn't even aware that Patrick and I had agreed to meet! – She had only been informed that Patrick had been found. Nothing else! – I think this is appalling.

During my long search for Margaret, the Irish authorities made it very difficult for me, mostly because their priorities were all about protecting the birth mother. Well, they are not protecting her over this, are they? – They are not even letting her know that her son and daughter have made contact. What is stopping me from telling Patrick where Margaret is, other than my conscience? And, if I told him, what could stop Patrick from showing up at her front door?

They really should have kept our birth mother in the loop. The poor woman is living in constant fear, every day of her life.

At any rate, I told Margaret that I had met Patrick and that he resembles her. I told her about his life so far and that he seemed very happy. She was grateful because, as she said, "The worst part about having babies and giving them away is the not knowing their whereabouts, or if they are happy and healthy – or even if they're still alive." She described it as being, "worse than a child dying, because when a child dies at least you know where they are. It was the not knowing for all those years that hurt the most". This touched me a great deal.

I mentioned that Patrick was eager to meet her – but she isn't ready for that. At this point, she still doubts that she will ever be able to tell her husband about my two brothers, because she feels ashamed at "allowing" herself to get pregnant – and for giving three babies away. I told her she shouldn't feel that way because she'd been young and vulnerable and manipulated by an older man. (Not sure this sunk in, though.)

We also spoke about my birth father. She opened up a bit more about him, appearing to feel more relaxed with me than she had at the meeting in Dublin. She told me his full name, the year he was born and the year he died. She described him as a very domineering and controlling man – a predator, as Mary had once called him. He had known he was having sex with an underage and insecure girl. He had known her background. In his eyes she had been a second-class citizen because she had been abandoned by her birth mother – tossed aside like a piece of trash.

I asked Margaret if her adoptive mum had known the type of man he was, though I seemed to remember that she hadn't. Apparently, Peter had behaved like a loving boyfriend in front of her parents, and had completely taken them in. All they had seen was a caring man, a man who showered their daughter with gifts, love and affection.

In reality, he'd only been interested in exploiting her, even dictating when she could go out and whom she could see. When she was 32 and first met Jack, Peter did everything in his power to split them up. He wanted no one else to have her. He wanted complete control over her life. Margaret still feels guilty for allowing Peter to do what he did to her over so many years, but I urged her not to, because she hadn't known any better. She even said she had feared he would have controlled my life and done who knows what to me – this did not bear thinking about!

On hearing this I found myself feeling, still more strongly, that I wanted to visit his grave. Seeing the gravestone with his name on it might make all this more real – perhaps even drive home to me what a lucky escape I'd had.

As we spoke, I felt very sad for Margaret. Her innocent teenage years had been taken away from her. She had never experienced young love. She would first have experienced love upon meeting Jack, after over fifteen years of being exploited by Peter.

As the phone call was drifting to an end, I could sense Margaret didn't want it to. I asked her if she wanted to meet me when I visited Ireland in the summer. She said very softly, "Yes, I do."

Thinking that Max and I should meet her and Jack in a location where she would feel comfortable, I suggested that the four of us could go for lunch in some place of her choosing. Margaret seemed very happy with this arrangement. She told me, "It would be nice to include Jack, because he's been so supportive – and I'd like to know Max". All I needed to do was to confirm a date nearer the time.

As I confided to my diary: *I am so pleased I spoke to Margaret today! I feel more comfortable with her and find it easier to talk to her and ask her questions about her past. And she comes across as more at ease with herself with me, too.*

Chapter 38

Shortly after this I received an email from Ben in the Adoption Authority, telling me that he was leaving the Authority to work for a charity in the private sector. This came as a disappointment to me, because I had hoped that he would carry on the search for my youngest brother. Ben said he had done all he could in terms of trying to locate my brother. However, he had spoken to his manager and they had both agreed that the file could be closed. He did say, however, that if another match came up on the register the file would be reopened, and a new social worker assigned to the case.

I was unsure how I felt about this. With the file closed, there wouldn't be any investigative work being done. A friend of mine suggested that I should ask that the file be left open because otherwise "it's put at the bottom of the pile". I emailed Ben to request that it to be left open, but it had already been closed. I decided to get in touch with the Authority after the summer holidays and demand that it be reopened.

As I wrote: *I will miss Ben. He was a very good social worker. He handled Patrick's situation very professionally and he was easy to talk to and a good listener. I wish him the very best of luck in his new role.*

Chapter 39

July 12th, 2017. Max, Alex and I have been planning our annual family trip to Ireland. We are heading over on July 18th. We're hoping to meet up with some friends and family – some of whom I haven't seen for 17 years! Max and I are also looking forward to meeting Margaret and Patrick again. (On separate occasions, though.)

I had texted Margaret four weeks before, to see if she still wanted to meet for lunch when we were in Ireland. She had asked if we could meet on July 21st, down in Portlaoise. Margaret sounded quite upbeat in her texts, which was lovely.

I had thought Great, arrangements made: It will be Margaret, Jack, Max and me for lunch. (It was a bit too soon for Alex.) I had also asked Margaret if she had heard from Mary. She hadn't: "Not since January time".

On July 3rd I received the following email.

3 Jul at 10:27 AM

Hi Alice,

I hope all is well with you and your family. Can you let me know if you plan to meet with Margaret this summer? You might recall that she expressed a preference to meet in Portlaoise, if it's still your plan to visit. I know it has been a while since we last spoke, but it is my recollection that you spoke about meeting her again in July sometime. If that is the case, we would need to be planning dates in advance to suit everyone. I have not been in contact with Margaret in relation to this and will wait until I hear from you before I contact her.

Regards

Mary

Imagine my reaction! I phoned Mary straightaway, explaining that Margaret and I had already made plans to meet in July with our husbands. I informed her that I had contacted Margaret and she'd seemed happy, relaxed and comfortable with our arrangements. I also told Mary that we did not need her to attend, as it was to be an informal lunch between the four of us. Mary seemed okay with this.

I was beginning to feel quite excited that Margaret and I were going to share lunch together without the formality of the social worker. At least, that was what I thought until I received the following email:

12 Jul at 2:14 PM

Hi Alice,

Just a quick update. I was chatting to Margaret today about your plans to meet her next Friday 21 July in Portlaoise. As Jack will no longer be accompanying her, Margaret has asked me if I could be there as a support to her. Would it be ok to meet at the Maldron Hotel, Portlaoise on Friday 21st July at 12 noon or thereabouts? How do you feel about this? Margaret is really looking forward to your both getting to know each other and to forming a friendship.

Can you let me know if this suits you and safe travel.

Kind regards

Mary

My response:

12 Jul at 4:37 PM

Hi Mary,

If it makes Margaret feel more comfortable then it's fine by me.

Alice

I did not feel very happy about it – but if it was what Margaret wanted, I had to respect that.

Chapter 40

It is Monday July 17th: the day before our family trip to Ireland. The last email I received from Mary arrived late on Wednesday the 12th of July. (Mary only works Monday, Tuesday and Wednesday.) I have been thinking about the email and discussing it with Max. I am not at all happy with the way Mary has hijacked Margaret's and my lunch meeting. I keep having visions of it turning into a counselling session.

I got myself into such a tizz that I phoned Mary. When we eventually spoke, I reiterated that I did not want the lunch to turn into a formal counselling session. She informed me that it would be a relaxed lunch between three women. I objected, explaining that Max would be attending, as had been originally arranged. Mary told me that Max was no longer invited because of "Margaret's state of mind. She'll be feeling vulnerable if the past was discussed".

I did my best to make it clear to Mary that Margaret and I had already agreed we would not discuss the past – that we would concentrate on moving forward. I had reassured Margaret in our telephone conversation back in May that I wouldn't bring up her past as I was quite happy with the information, she had already given me. I had also reassured Margaret that Max would not dream of mentioning either Patrick or my other, unknown, brother.

I also told Margaret that I couldn't really ask Max to drive across Ireland, to a part of the country he didn't know, only to be asked to sit in another café and wait for us to finish. It was particularly unfair to ask this of him after Margaret had already agreed to his being there. Mary then asked if Max would be willing to sit out the first thirty minutes of the meeting, so that she could calm Margaret's nerves. I made it clear that I wasn't very happy with this arrangement but reluctantly agreed. At the end of the conversation I stressed, yet again, that I did not want a formal meeting and that I wanted to concentrate on moving forward. Mary agreed to this.

Chapter 41

On July 21st Max and I drove to Portlaoise, a two-hour drive from my mum's, leaving Alex to stay with his cousins and to learn about farming for the day.

Max and I made it to the meeting place in time at noon. As we approached the hotel, I spotted Mary and Margaret already sitting in a booth. Upon seeing us, Mary quickly made her way to the doorway and asked Max if he would go next door to the café, which he did.

As soon as I sat down in the booth, I knew I wasn't in for a relaxed lunch. I said hello to Margaret, who looked well but a little nervous. Mary and Margaret had already had tea and scones; I took a deep breath and ordered a coffee.

Mary started the conversation by saying "Alice, I believe you've met Patrick since you've been home?" I replied, rather startled, that I had. She said, "Have you a photograph to show Margaret?" I proceeded to show Margaret the photograph, commenting on how much Patrick resembled her. As soon as Margaret saw the photograph she broke down. She was absolutely inconsolable – so distressed that Mary took her outside.

I really don't think Mary had helped Margaret at all. She should have eased Patrick into the conversation, allowing us both to reacquaint ourselves before discussing anything potentially distressing for her. Margaret should have been made to feel relaxed and secure. She wasn't.

Twenty-five minutes later I was still sitting on my own. I texted Max and he urged me to sit tight for five more minutes. (I was tempted to leave, especially as Mary hadn't even come back to let me know how Margaret was doing.) I agreed to wait, but I felt very unhappy. To me, the meeting had disaster written all over it. It was certainly not the relaxed lunch Margaret and I had envisaged when we had arranged it back in May.

Thirty minutes later, Mary returned. She said, "Margaret has composed herself and we're now convening in the hotel lobby." I followed Mary, with some misgivings, to a very public lobby. It consisted of a reception desk, a small two-seater sofa, a chair and low table. The lifts to the bedrooms were opposite. There was a narrow walkway between us and the lifts. It was all very cramped. This was not an ideal place to have our meeting. We could also be heard from every angle.

Mary started the conversation by asking Margaret various things about her past. I could instantly see that this was upsetting to Margaret – so I hastily reminded Mary that we had covered Margaret's past when we had last met. I also mentioned that

Margaret and I wanted to concentrate on moving forward. I hoped Mary would get the hint – that we neither wanted nor needed to go over old ground. Unfortunately, everything I said fell on deaf ears.

What Mary did next was unforgivable.

She turned to Margaret and said, "Is there something you want to tell Alice?" Upon hearing this question, Margaret suddenly couldn't make eye contact with me. As she hesitated, I interrupted, saying, "I don't think I need to know this."

Ignoring me, Mary asked her a second time. Then Margaret started to tell her story – very reluctantly, I must say. She couldn't even bring herself to look at me, which surprised me less after I'd heard what she had to say.

Out of respect for Margaret I am not going to repeat her story here. I am simply going to state that it had absolutely no relevance to our relationship. It was an incident that affected her immediate family only. In fact, I'm still flabbergasted to think that Mary felt the need to request that Margaret share this with me – especially as it only upset Margaret even more – and she was in a fragile enough state as it was!

After Margaret had finished it was obvious that she was upset, but Mary still did not back off. She proceeded to ply Margaret with more and more questions about her past. She asked her how she felt when her son was born, when her granddaughter had been born. . . What sort of questions were these? Margaret had an embarrassed, almost hunted, look. She answered the question about her granddaughter by saying – again – that when she'd held her she had been transported back to the day when she'd taken me to Dublin and handed me over to the nuns, under Clerys Clock.

It was at this point that I decided, singlehandedly, to end the meeting. This was not what I had wanted, and certainly not what I'd come for. I felt that Margaret's whole being – all the self-respect that she had managed to build up over the years was in tatters – and all because Mary kept raking up the past! By doing this Mary had managed to traumatise this poor woman! She was forcing her to relive her nightmares and face her demons again and again. I was quite disgusted.

Remember: this discussion was going on in a very public place, a very inappropriate place, in my opinion. Also, I had not agreed, either to the topics of discussion or to the formality of the meeting. We should have been having lunch, talking about moving forward and forming a friendship. We should have been chatting about our families and showing photographs.

This was not a relaxed lunch between three women. This was a box-ticking exercise by a social worker with an agenda.

When I left, I felt that this was probably the last I would ever hear from Margaret. She did not *need* all this, at her time of life. And . . . whatever would she tell her husband Jack about the meeting? She would have to lie to him and pretend that everything had gone well - and the strain would probably be obvious.

He would probably say, "Not sure that these meetings with your daughter are doing you much good" – and that would be the end of it.

Chapter 42

I arrived back in the UK on July 23rd. Since that day, I can't seem to get Margaret and that dreadful meeting out of my mind. I keep thinking about the humiliation she suffered. The image I keep recalling is that of a fragile little old woman distraught at having to relive, unnecessarily, the memories and nightmares she had endured decades before.

After a lot of thinking and discussing with Max I decided to write a letter of complaint to Mary's team leader, highlighting Mary's treatment of Margaret on July 21st.

Nora,

Regarding the meeting dated 21st July 2017 between Margaret, Mary and me, I am writing to express my anger at the manner of the handling of the meeting.

Margaret and I had slowly developed contact by text and phone since our initial meeting. Information about the past and our current lives had been freely discussed and it was agreed that a lunch meeting between ourselves and our partners would be appropriate when I came over to Ireland with my family.

As far as I was concerned all my questions had been answered and Margaret had even indicated that she would direct me to the burial place of my birth father at the next meeting, which represented the final piece of the jigsaw for me. Lunch on the 21st July was agreed and my impression was Margaret was looking forward to it, as a way of looking towards the future.

A subsequent call from Mary indicated she would be present as Margaret's husband Jack was unable to attend and Margaret was worried about facing myself and Max alone. I reiterated to Mary to please convey to Margaret that she need not be concerned, as in my opinion we were looking forward, not to the past. When advised that my husband would no longer be welcome I considered cancelling the meeting as I strongly felt this was to be a social meeting, not a formal one, and that it would be unfair for him to be omitted, having driven me across the country to meet Margaret. The compromise reached was that Max would not attend the first 30 minutes of the lunch.

I feel very unhappy about the way this meeting was hijacked by Mary. It was steered by an agenda that was certainly not mine, nor did I feel that Margaret was in any way driving it.

I must also strongly object to the way Mary led the meeting.

She immediately began going over old ground, racking up the past when there was no call for it, and refusing to allow Margaret and me to move forward. There was one aspect of the meeting that was totally inappropriate, when Mary felt that Margaret should advise me of a private family issue, something concerning her son, my half brother. This bore absolutely no relevance, either to our meeting or to the future, and it was also clearly embarrassing for Margaret. The matter was private, between Margaret and her immediate family, and to have aired it at a meeting between Margaret and me was a horrendous act by a single individual under your stewardship.

Mary was not privy to the text and phone conversations between myself and Margaret and yet she still saw fit to push an agenda that was wholly inappropriate and completely at odds with where my birth mother and I had moved to. It seemed to me to be yet another example of your department's obsession with the need for counselling, whether the individuals involved requested it, needed it or even wanted it.

Mary also touched upon my brother Patrick, whom I have traced and subsequently met. Margaret was aware of this (from our private conversations) but this was not supposed to be a topic of conversation on the 21st July.

I have been very wary of discussing Patrick with Margaret and had only previously responded to prompts for information from Margaret. However, Mary immediately launched into discussing Patrick at the meeting. Margaret appeared traumatised by this, and the meeting was paused for 25 minutes while she attempted to regain composure. Also: Margaret had not asked to see his photo, but Mary requested that it be shown. Why was the photo on Mary's agenda when it was irrelevant to the ongoing relationship between me and Margaret?

The meeting bore no resemblance to what Margaret and I had planned, proved totally unsatisfactory from my perspective and seemed to be completely traumatic for Margaret. Why such a meeting was held – and in such a public area – is beyond me. The sole responsibility for this lies with Mary, her wholly inappropriate agenda and the way in which she led the meeting.

I am at a loss to understand why Mary had to be at the meeting at all and will certainly not be informing her of any future meetings with Margaret. If Margaret chooses to inform her, that is her prerogative, but I will not be attending any future meetings involving a member of your department.

I request that a note be placed on the file that I no longer wish to be contacted by the department in any way. In my opinion, your role was to facilitate the meetings of adoptees with birth parents, should both parties wish it. The actions by your employee demonstrated an air of arrogance that is wholly inappropriate, and one I hope you investigate with vigour.

Alice

I sent a second email asking Nora to acknowledge receipt of the complaint. I received acknowledgement on July 26th. In the email Nora said that she would look into it, but that she would be unable to get back to me for four weeks, as various people are on holiday. So, I had to play the waiting game.

Chapter 43

Today I decided to phone Margaret to see how she was. Somehow, I had the feeling that Mary had not phoned her since that awful meeting. Surprise, surprise: I was right. How can a social worker fail to follow up on the welfare of a client – especially one as distressed as Margaret had been?

I spoke to Margaret for the best part of an hour. She was very apologetic about the meeting. Straightaway I told her she had nothing to apologise for. I asked her how she was feeling after Friday. She wasn't really in a good place mentally because she'd had to deal with the trauma of the meeting and then go home to Jack and pretend that everything was okay. She had been unable to speak to anyone about what had happened because she had no one to confide in. She had been carrying such a heavy load on her shoulders! – I really do not know how she hadn't gone insane.

I told Margaret about my complaint to Mary's team leader. I explained how angry I was at how Mary had treated her. All the pain and heartache of that day could so easily have been avoided! Margaret admitted that she hadn't understood why Max hadn't been there: she hadn't realised that Mary had asked him to stay away, and that, at first, she'd been disappointed that he "hadn't come". I told Margaret that Mary had made it quite clear that Max was not welcome.

I also mentioned how sorry I was that she'd had to endure the ordeal of telling me about her son's situation, when there had been no need.

Margaret told me she was with Mary for a further two hours after I left. During this time, Mary had told her that she thought I did not show "any warmth" towards Margaret. That everything was "very strained". That I was "cold" and "lacked feeling". (I still cannot believe all this, even as I'm writing it!)

Mary had even told Margaret that she did not think she would hear from me again. She said that Margaret didn't have to accept my phone calls or reply to my texts. She could sever all communication with me if she wanted to. My blood boiled as I heard this. What part of Mary's job was it, to plant negative seeds in Margaret's mind?

As I wrote later: Mary has behaved despicably – as well as completely unprofessionally – and the bottom line is, I have to do something to stop this social worker from treating others in this manner ever again. I have written a follow-up letter of complaint to Nora, after my conversation with Margaret.

To

Nora

26 Jul at 7:04 PM

Thank you for confirming receipt of the emails.

I must make you aware that the situation has developed in the last 24 hours, after I made a courtesy call to Margaret. I want to make the following points to you as a result:

1. Margaret has not been contacted at all since our meeting by your department, despite being clearly traumatised during the meeting. In fact, Margaret was with Mary for a further two hours going through all the issues, even after I left. Margaret is an old lady and no heed appears to have been paid to the fact that she then had to drive herself home and face questions from her husband, Jack.

2. Margaret was unaware that Max had been excluded from the meeting, at Mary's request. She also told me that she had agreed to Mary's presence only at Mary's insistence. (Mary had told me that Margaret had requested her presence as a prerequisite to the meeting going forward.)

3. Margaret would not have divulged the private family issue to me had Mary not prompted her. It was not by her desire that this issue was raised.

4. Mary told Margaret that I showed a lack of warmth during the meeting and Margaret left the meeting feeling that she and I would likely be no longer in contact, which was a great disappointment to her. I totally refute this inference. Mary never let either of us express ourselves, insisted upon our focussing on issues that neither of us wished to discuss again and expected us to be open and vocal in what amounted to a public place.

5. Margaret was even advised by Mary not to feel pressurised into accepting a phone call from me – which amounted to overtly discouraging Margaret in continuing our new relationship.

I have now reiterated to Margaret that I would like the friendship to be given a chance to develop and we have agreed to meet again (with partners) the next time we are in Ireland, allowing us the opportunity to move forward. Margaret said that she was pleased at that.

As for Mary: her behaviour has been, quite simply, unprofessional. She has interfered beyond her remit and against the wishes of both parties, creating issues where they need not have arisen and generating upset when it could have been avoided.

I strongly urge that Mary no longer contacts Margaret and that you, as a team leader, reflect on the poor light this episode places on your department, at a time when your reputation is already under pressure in the national eye.

Alice

April 15, 2018

As the months have passed, I have kept in contact with both Margaret and Patrick. I have spoken to Margaret a couple of times on the telephone and we have also had some text conversations. She is still very nervous about her husband and her son's finding out about Patrick and my other blood brother. She still fears both might disown her if her secrets ever came out.

Having said that, Margaret is very chatty when I phone her. She seems to open up more about her past and appears more relaxed with me. This may be because I phone when Jack is at work and she doesn't have to be careful with what she's saying. She never asks about Patrick. I still feel she is in denial of his existence.

Margaret seems to be very happy and in a good place in her life. For that reason, I am having reservations about meeting her and Jack when I go to Ireland in the summer. I do know she really wants to meet Alex, but I am very nervous about Max or Alex letting something slip about Patrick. I could not live with myself if I was responsible for Margaret's losing her family! – So, I have decided that the best way forward for Margaret and me at present is by conversing via text or telephone instead.

I have also been in touch with Patrick over the last few months – or rather, he's been in touch with me! He has texted and phoned quite a lot. In fact, he's become a bit obsessive, which is unnerving. He talks about me to his friends and when we meet, he puts me on display for everyone to see. It is quite embarrassing.

He has even been to England to see me – just showed up at our home, without giving me any notice. That was unsettling too. Every time we speak, whether in person or by phone, he asks me about Margaret. Each time I tell him what I know. He is always asking me if she might meet him. I tell him no, because of her circumstances. But – he doesn't seem to retain the information I give him. That may be because he appears to have a drink problem. This became very apparent recently, when Max and I met him and his wife Sarah, in Dublin.

As Max has pointed out, Patrick's drinking issue appears worse each time we've met him. It was so bad on the last occasion that I have reluctantly decided to sever all ties with him for the moment. I simply do not feel that he is in a responsible place.

Having said that, upon looking back over the past four years, I feel immensely proud of what I achieved. I am so glad to have found Margaret and so grateful that she has given me answers to questions I have waited my whole life to hear. I hope and trust that, in the not-so-distant future, Margaret and I can meet again in person without dark clouds hanging over us: fears that her life might be upended, fears that Patrick might do something disastrous.

I have come so far – it has not been easy, but I have had such support!

I would never have been able to complete this journey without Max's love and patience. He has kept me focussed and given me the determination to carry on. Both Max and Alex have been my strength.

There were also no limits to the support I received from my mum and sister. My sister gave me the strength to stand up to Mary. She served as my private investigator, assistant and driver. She was always there for me when I needed her. I was so grateful to her – and to them all.

Who knows what the future holds? I suspect that the journey that began 48 years ago underneath Clerys clock has yet to run its course. However – with the support and love of my family – I'm ready for it.

Appendix

Post Adoption Information Leaflet: Adopted people No 9

Council of Irish Adoption Agencies

Preparing for a meeting with your birth mother or birth father

It is recommended that you avail of the support and assistance of your adoption agency if you are planning to meet with your birth mother or birth father. A reunion meeting is a complex emotional process. Part of the social worker's role is to offer support to all those involved and to mediate and facilitate contact.

Studies have shown that a reunion can be a very positive experience even when it does not lead to an ongoing relationship. Generally, those who meet consider that there are more advantages than disadvantages to meeting. Those who have met gain more knowledge about the other person and often experience a sense of healing as a result.

There are many issues that you should consider prior to your meeting. It may be one of the most significant events in your life and in the lives of those around you. It is therefore important to prepare for the initial meeting by considering the following:

- Why do you want to meet?
- What are your expectations of meeting your birth mother/birth father?
- How might the reunion affect the people you care about?
- Do you have someone you trust with whom you can discuss your hopes and expectations of this meeting?
- Are you prepared to be mindful of your birth mother's/birth father's feelings?
- Are you prepared to receive information which you may find difficult to accept? How might you handle this information?
- Have you thought about how you will accept your birth mother's/birth father's

feelings, choices, lifestyles, if they are different from yours?

• What are your supports to help you cope if you are disappointed with the outcome of the reunion?

• How might it be if your birth mother/birth father wants a closer relationship than you anticipated or are ready for?

Further questions to reflect on:

• How will you feel if your birth mother/birth father has not told anybody about you and may not be ready or willing to do so?

• Are you prepared for the fact that the contact with your birth mother/birth father may be set at her/his pace?

• How will you feel if your birth mother has placed other children for adoption?

• Are you prepared for the different ways your siblings might react?

• Are you prepared for the different ways your birth parent's partner might react?

• How would you feel if your birth parents married each other and had more children?

CIAA 2012 1

Post Adoption Information Leaflet: Adopted people No 9

• How would you feel if your birth parents were not ready or willing to tell your half/full-siblings about you?

• How would you react if you were told difficult or sensitive information regarding your conception and/or birth? For example, if the pregnancy was the result of non-consensual sexual relationship, incest or an extra-marital relationship.

• How would you feel if you learned that there are health issues in your birth family history, for example, mental health concerns, physical disabilities and/or genetic conditions?

- How would you feel if you learned that there is a history of alcohol or drug addiction?

- How would you feel if you learned that your birth parent had engaged in criminal behaviour?

- Are you aware of the issue of genetic sexual attraction?

The following steps can be useful before a first meeting:

- It is generally advised that first names only are used in letters during the early stages and that identifying details are not given. It is easier to share identifying information when both of you are happy and comfortable with the developing relationship. During this time of exchange of information and letter writing, take the opportunity to discuss with your social worker what identifying information you are comfortable sharing so as to ensure that your confidentiality is protected in case at some stage you decide that you do not wish to continue to have contact.

- Exchange of information – this can include a résumé of life events. This can be useful in bringing each person up-to-date on the other's life, and past and present circumstances. It can be helpful to have such information before a first meeting.
- Exchanging letters, photographs, tapes, dvds/video before a first meeting.

Photographs or dvds are a way of getting to know the person you are meeting. However not everyone will be comfortable with sharing photographs. Letters may give an opportunity to ask/answer some questions and to build up some information.

Remember not everyone finds writing easy so you will need to take this into account both for yourself and for your birth parent(s).

Planning for a first meeting:

The plan and structure of the meeting should be discussed with your social worker and it is best if these details are agreed by everyone beforehand.

Who attends?

Usually the first meeting is between you and the birth parent you have searched for. It is important that an opportunity is created for the people directly concerned to meet each other first.

How long should the meeting last?

This is hard to decide, but generally about 2 hours is a good rule of thumb. Because the first reunion meeting is an emotional event for everyone, it is important that you have enough time but also that it is not overwhelming. If your meeting is being facilitated by a social worker, he/she will offer to check in with you during the meeting, and you can decide if you feel this would be helpful.
CIAA 2012 2

Post Adoption Information Leaflet: Adopted people No 9

What else will help?

It will be important also to think about the following:

Discuss where the meeting will take place. Your social worker will consult both of you and a decision will be reached regarding the location of the meeting.
It will be important that the time you meet is arranged so that one person will plan to arrive earlier than the other person. Be sure you set it up so that you do not meet in the reception area of a building.

Discuss with your social worker prior to the meeting what information you are happy to share, or not yet ready to share with your birth mother or birth father.

Decide if you would like to have the social worker with you to make initial introductions.

Some people like to bring a small gift, but this is not essential. Discuss this with your social worker before the meeting in order to see what might be best in your particular situation.

Recognise that everyone will be nervous. Be yourself, use first names and try to relax.

Consider bringing along some photographs. These can help to start and keep conversations going as you relate stories from the photographs.

You may wish to bring a camera to your first meeting. It is a good idea to discuss this with your social worker so that you can find out if your birth parent is okay to have photographs taken.

Be aware of both your own and your birth parent's need for privacy and be prepared for the fact that there may be some difficult or private issues which will not be discussed at the first meeting.

It is important that the first meeting ends in a planned way. The ending of the meeting, especially if you are not sure what will happen next, can be very difficult and emotional for everyone involved.

The first meeting can bring up emotions and feelings that you may not have expected or been prepared for. It is important to give yourself time to reflect on this first meeting. It is not advisable to rush into making plans for further meetings at this stage. Take some time out to decide if and how you would like to proceed with contact.

At the end of the meeting it is a good idea for you both to contact the social worker to organise the next meeting if that is what you have agreed. Alternatively, if you have agreed to share your phone numbers you can arrange further meetings directly with your birth parent.

Arrange some support for yourself. It is not advised to return directly to work or to college after the reunion. Many meetings can be emotionally exhausting for everyone involved. Take time out either by yourself or with a friend or family member.

The first meeting may be different from what you had expected. You may need some support and a chance to reflect on the experience and your feelings afterwards. Sometimes it can be disappointing for one or both parties, particularly where one or the other has expectations of a warm relationship that is not shared by the other person. Your social worker will provide support for you and may be able to put you in touch with others who have had experiences similar to your own.

CIAA 2012 3

Post Adoption Information Leaflet: Adopted people No 9

The support of your social worker will continue to be available to you for as long as you wish after the reunion, so you should feel at ease asking for this help if you need it.

Acknowledgements

Thank you to my husband for always being there for me especially through the dark times.

Thank you to my son for being patient and understanding.

Thank you to my editor, Alice McVeigh, for helping me put my story out there for you to read and benefit from.

Printed in Great Britain
by Amazon